"You have your fantasies and I have mine..."

"You're even prettier than I remembered." Jake swallowed. "We stripped down so fast and then didn't put on clothes until morning."

Amethyst slipped her arms around his neck. "I couldn't get enough of you."

"We couldn't get enough of each other." As he caressed her, he leaned down, his lips nearly making contact. "And this would be the moment when normally I'd kiss you and thrust my tongue deep into your inviting wet mouth. But I can't."

Desire poured like lava through her veins. "There are other places you can kiss me."

"I know. That was my plan." His voice was thick with anticipation. Then he dropped to his knees and braced his hands on either side of her shoulders. "I loved having you tell me what you like. Tell me again."

His voice grew husky. "Hearing you say what you want gets me hot."

Dear Reader,

Season's greetings from Thunder Mountain Ranch! I see that the big tree is up in the living room and somebody's stringing Christmas lights along the front porch. Hey, who's that pulling into the drive in a big black truck? Must be Jake Ramsey! He's taken a few days off from his firefighting job in Jackson Hole so he can spend the holidays with his foster parents.

You'll enjoy meeting Jake, because a cowboy who's also a firefighter has hero potential coming out his ears. Think about it. He chose a profession that involves charging into burning buildings to save people and animals. That takes courage and compassion, plus a lot of lovely muscles. Oh, and whenever he's not in uniform, he wears jeans, boots and a Stetson. It's no wonder Amethyst Ferguson wants some quality time with Jake while he's in town!

Welcome to another sexy adventure in the Thunder Mountain Brotherhood series. If you've read the preceding books, you'll be excited to get a glimpse of some of your favorite characters gathered around the Christmas tree. But if you're new to the series, never fear! I'll make sure you won't be confused about who's who and what's what. It'll be a memorable holiday at the ranch, and I can't wait to share it with you!

Merry Christmas to all,

Vicki Lewis Thompson

Vicki Lewis Thompson

Cowboy Unwrapped

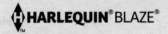

Recycling programs
for this product may
not exist in your area.

ISBN-13 978-0-373-79923-7

Cowboy Unwrapped

Copyright © 2016 by Vicki Lewis Thompson

Printed in U.S.A.

www.Harlequin.com

A passion for travel has taken *New York Times* bestselling author **Vicki Lewis Thompson** to Europe, Great Britain, the Greek isles, Australia and New Zealand. She's visited most of North America and has her eye on South America's rain forests. Africa, India and China beckon. But her first love is her home state of Arizona, with its deserts, mountains, sunsets and—last but not least—cowboys! The wide-open spaces and heroes on horseback influence everything she writes. Connect with her at vickilewisthompson.com, Facebook.com/vickilewisthompson and Twitter.com/vickilthompson.

Books by Vicki Lewis Thompson

Harlequin Blaze

Thunder Mountain Brotherhood

Midnight Thunder
Thunderstruck
Rolling Like Thunder
A Cowboy Under the Mistletoe
Cowboy All Night
Cowboy After Dark
Cowboy Untamed

Sons of Chance

Cowboys & Angels
Riding High
Riding Hard
Riding Home
A Last Chance Christmas

To get the inside scoop on Harlequin Blaze and its talented writers, visit Facebook.com/BlazeAuthors.

All backlist available in ebook format.

Visit the Author Profile page
at Harlequin.com for more titles.

For Isabeau the cat, 1994–2016. What a serene, happy soul. You will be missed.

1

WHEN JAKE RAMSEY pulled into the circular gravel drive in front of Thunder Mountain Ranch at sundown, he thought he'd stumbled onto the set of *National Lampoon's Christmas Vacation*. His foster brothers Cade Gallagher and Finn O'Roarke stood in the freezing cold struggling to untangle a string of Christmas lights while wearing thick gloves. Why they needed more lights was a mystery because the low-slung ranch house already looked as if Clark Griswold had been there.

Happy as Jake was to see those two cowboys after all this time away, his firefighter training took precedence over a sentimental reunion. He'd bet a month's pay neither of them had bothered to check the UL ratings to see if the fuse box could take another strand of what looked like incandescent bulbs. Hadn't they heard of LEDs? And was that an *indoor* extension cord connected to the net lights on a bush by the porch? Jesus.

He wondered if Damon Harrison had approved this setup. Damon, Cade and Finn had been the original three taken in by Rosie and Herb Padgett years ago when they'd decided to make the ranch a foster home for teenage boys. Cade had become a horse trainer who worked at the ranch, now a residential equine education center for older teens, called Thunder Mountain Academy. Finn had moved to Seattle and opened his own microbrewery. Those jobs didn't qualify either of them to handle electrical installations.

But Damon and Philomena, who'd married this past summer, renovated houses here in Sheridan. Jake doubted they'd been involved in this fustercluck. It had Cade written all over it. The guy was great with horses but not so great with a toolbox.

Cade and Finn glanced up as he pulled up next to them in his F-250. They wouldn't recognize the truck because he'd bought it since his last visit home in early March. Plus he hadn't seen Finn in years. Finn and his fiancée Chelsea were spending Christmas at the ranch, which had added to Jake's excitement about his first Christmas home since getting hired by the Jackson Hole Fire Department.

From the looks of things, they needed him here. Cade and Finn were fixing to burn down the house. He shut off the engine and climbed out, making sure his boots didn't slip on the ice he knew would be under the thin layer of snow covering the driveway.

Then he buttoned his sheepskin coat against the wind and crammed his Stetson a little tighter on his head before walking around the front of the truck. He could see his breath. That was another stupid thing—putting up Christmas lights when the temperature was near zero.

"Hey, bozos," he called out to Cade and Finn, who'd stopped what they were doing while they waited to see who'd driven up. "Why don't you let someone who knows what he's doing handle that job?"

"Jake?" Cade dropped his end of the lights into the snow and hurried toward him. "You got a new truck, man!"

"That I did." He exchanged a hug with Cade.

"Jake Ramsey?" Finn tossed his end away and came over. "I haven't seen your ugly mug since I left for Seattle! How the hell are you?"

Jake returned his hug. "I'm good, real good. Hated that I had to miss Damon's wedding, but a couple of guys got sick and I couldn't leave."

"You would've loved it," Cade said. "It rained like hell, the wind destroyed most of the decorations and we had to delay the ceremony until the storm passed. Then we had to stand in the mud while Damon and Phil said their vows. It was epic."

"Sounds awesome. Wish I'd been there. Speaking of the happy couple, where are they?"

"Wimping out in Florida with the in-laws," Finn said. "They'll be back tomorrow, looking all tanned and smug while the rest of us are the color of grubworms."

"Real Wyoming cowboys don't go to Florida for a winter vacation." Cade tucked his gloved hands into his armpits and stomped his feet in the snow. "They tough it out like manly men."

"Damn straight," Finn said. "But I'm thinking we should tough it out inside by the fire for a while and finish this project in the morning. We don't want to keep poor Jake standing out here shivering. He needs to head in and see the folks."

"I want to see them, too," Jake said, "but I have a question before we go in. Did you guys put up all these lights?"

Cade grinned at him. "You're impressed, right? You

didn't think we could do it without Damon around to help, but there's the evidence." Cade swept an arm to encompass the glittering front of the house. "Damon's gonna shit a brick when he sees this."

"That's for sure." Jake walked over and fingered the indoor extension cord. "I take it you ran out of outdoor cords."

"Yeah, but those work fine." Finn shrugged. "We bought a bunch of extra lights and forgot about getting more cords, but we found those in the barn. They're a little worn but we wound electrical tape around the parts where wires were sticking out."

Jake did his best to control himself. "How many of these are you using?"

"I don't know," Cade said. "Six, maybe seven. We're almost done, but I agree with Finn. We can quit now and finish up tomorrow. We have time before Damon and Phil get back."

"You know what?" Jake was proud of himself. He didn't yell and he didn't cuss, although he desperately wanted to do both. "Before I go in, let me take a quick run into town. With tomorrow being the last shopping day, the hardware store should be open. I'll just pick up a few outdoor extension cords."

"Ah, don't bother." Cade fished one end of the light strand out of the snow and began winding it around his arm. "Extra trouble, extra expense and for what?"

"Oh, I don't know." Jake kept his tone casual. "Maybe to keep those frayed extension cords from setting the house on fire."

Cade blinked. "We put electrical tape around them. That should do it."

"Hey, he's a firefighter." Finn clapped Cade on the

shoulder. "We should probably let him do his thing. I admit those cords are a little dicey."

Jake shuddered to think what they looked like. They'd probably been moldering in the barn for years. No doubt varmints had chewed on them. "I've seen the result of using frayed cords," he said. "I'd sleep better knowing I've replaced them. They're not designed for outdoor use, anyway, although the UL rating label is probably gone by now."

Finn exchanged a glance with Cade.

"Don't worry," Cade said in a low voice. "They're fine."

"What?" Jake didn't like the sound of that. "What's fine?"

Cade finished winding the strand around his arm. "Some of the lights were on sale. The labels said for indoor use only, but they were really reasonable so I thought if we put them on the porch—"

"Holy hell, Cade!" Jake finally lost it. "Are you telling me even the lights aren't rated for outdoor use?"

"A few, but—"

"Okay, here's what we're going to do. I'll drive into town and pick up a whole bunch of outdoor extension cords and more lights with the proper rating. In the morning I'll help you and Finn replace those extension cords and indoor lights. In the meantime, I want you to turn off everything."

Cade looked as if he wanted to argue.

"I know you think I'm an anal safety nut, but last week I hauled a single mom and her two little kids out of a house fire caused by frayed extension cords."

Finn sighed. "I hate to say it, but he's right, bro." He

dug in his pocket. "Let me donate some cash toward that purchase, Jake."

"Nah, my treat." Jake waved off the money. "I didn't know what to give the folks for Christmas so I was going to buy something after I got here. I'll just make this my gift."

Cade nodded. "Okay, I bow to your superior knowledge regarding decorative lighting. But can I make a small request?"

"Sure."

"Could you not mention any of this to Damon and Phil? The folks will have to know since this'll be your Christmas present, but Damon would never let me hear the end of it."

"I'll be silent as the tomb."

"Good. Oh, and that goes for Lexi, too. She's attending an indoor riding clinic and won't be back in town until tomorrow, either. My goal was to surprise all three of them with an awesome display."

"We'll do that, I promise." Jake knew how much Cade wanted to please Lexi, the love of his life. "It'll look just as fantastic as it does now, only it'll be safe."

Cade's gusty exhale created a cloud of vapor. "Thanks." He glanced back at the house. "I'm guessing nobody heard you drive up since they didn't come out, so you can probably just go and they won't be the wiser."

"Perfect. I'll make this quick."

"Dinner's at six-thirty," Finn said. "Tuna casserole."

"Hot damn. I'll be back in time." He left them, rounded the truck and climbed in behind the wheel, but he didn't pull away until the Christmas lights had winked out. Only then did the muscles in his neck and shoulders relax. Disaster averted.

The road into Sheridan had been recently plowed so he made good time, accompanied by the sultry voice of Amethyst Ferguson on his truck stereo. In his opinion she sounded way better than Katy Perry or Taylor Swift, but then again, he could be prejudiced. And he still hadn't decided what to do about her. Initially he'd planned to send her a text saying he'd be in town for a few days, but then he'd reconsidered.

He'd be busy with his foster family and she'd probably be busy with her folks, too, assuming she wasn't performing somewhere. If she happened to be out of town that would settle his dilemma, but he couldn't find that out without contacting her. He'd hate knowing she was here only to discover that family obligations would prevent them from having any private time.

And that's what he was hoping for. Last summer she'd had a gig at a resort in Jackson Hole and he'd caught her final show. Because he hadn't seen her since their PG-rated dates in high school, he'd invited her for drinks afterward. Sure enough, they'd reignited the spark and had spent the rest of the night in her hotel room.

The sex had been super hot, but they'd agreed that her budding career, his demanding schedule and the miles between Sheridan and Jackson Hole would keep them from meeting on a regular basis. They'd made no definite plans. If she had another gig in Jackson Hole she'd let him know, and if he paid a visit to his foster parents he'd give her a shout.

But this was a special holiday, not some random long weekend. He hadn't spent Christmas at the Last Chance in years due to his rookie status at the fire station. Finally he could look forward to celebrating with his foster parents and any foster brothers who showed up.

That could turn into a crowd. Because of the holidays, the Thunder Mountain Academy students had cleared out of the log cabins down in the meadow. Finn and Chelsea had likely claimed one and Jake had figured on taking another one but that left two more plus guest rooms in the ranch house.

Although his foster mom used to make a big pot of vegetable soup on Christmas Eve, she'd told him on the phone that she'd decided to have a buffet this year. But the tradition of opening presents after the meal would continue as always. Christmas Day was filled with card games, basketball on TV, snowball fights in the yard and a turkey dinner. He didn't want to miss any of that.

On the other hand, he'd thought about Amethyst fairly often during these past few months. He'd downloaded all of her music and played it quite a bit. The prospect of seeing her again affected his pulse rate. Imagining another night like they'd spent last summer sent all his blood south.

Yeah, he had a little fixation going on when it came to Amethyst Ferguson, whereas she might have put him right out of her mind. Besides, she'd mentioned sharing a house with her sister and he'd be at the ranch with a whole lot of people around. The cabins were set up with bunk beds, so even if he invited Amethyst to spend the night with him, it wouldn't be the luxurious and intimate setup they'd had in Jackson Hole.

He should probably forget trying to connect with her and concentrate on enjoying his first Christmas home in years. While Jackson looked great for the holidays, Sheridan had its own small-town charm. He'd always loved how the old-fashioned lampposts looked when they were decorated. As he'd predicted, the hardware store was still open. The extension cords should be in stock but he wondered if the lights would be picked over. If so, they'd just make do with fewer lights.

He found a parking spot and pulled in. Last-minute shoppers with colorful Christmas bags hurried along the sidewalk. He was glad for an excuse to come into town and be part of the bustling scene. Thanks to his foster parents and his years at Thunder Mountain, he'd learned to love the season.

Displays of gift ideas dominated the front of the store and he paused to look at a selection of smoke alarms. Last time he'd visited the ranch he'd worried that the ones in the house weren't top of the line. If he bought these for the folks, then he wouldn't have to announce that the extension cords were his gift and Cade could save face. Matter of fact, he could buy smoke alarms for everyone on his list. An extra one was always helpful and then he wouldn't have to come back into town tomorrow to Christmas shop.

"Typical fireman, mesmerized by the beauty of smoke alarms."

He turned around and there stood Amethyst with a smile on her face and a sparkle of laughter in her blue eyes. She wore a red knit cap pulled over her dark hair and a red coat with a furry collar. His heart kicked into high gear and he couldn't think of a single thing to say.

"Thought you could sneak into town, did you?" There was a teasing note in her voice.

He remembered how she liked to tease, especially in bed. "No! I was going to contact you, but then I thought about your family and how you probably wouldn't have time, so—"

"I understand." Her gaze gentled. "I was kidding you. It's not like we had an ironclad agreement. Christmas *is* busy."

"But I'd love to spend time with you." He couldn't help saying it. She looked more beautiful than ever and he had vivid memories of how she felt in his arms. He wanted her there again.

"I'd love to spend time with you, too." The flicker of awareness in her eyes sent an unmistakable message.

It went straight to his groin. "But I don't know when. Tonight's out. I just got here."

"I couldn't anyway. Family dinner."

"And tomorrow night's Christmas Eve. That's a big deal at the ranch. Maybe you'd like to come out there?"

"That's a possibility. Our big celebration is on Christmas Day. But I'd need to check with my folks and see what's planned. You know how it is."

"Absolutely. That's why I didn't contact you. I knew it could be dicey."

"True, but there has to be some free time." She brightened. "Maybe tomorrow during the day?"

He was encouraged by her eagerness to see him. "I have some stuff to do with the guys in the morning, but how about tomorrow afternoon? If you'd be willing to drive out to the ranch in the early afternoon, we could—" He thought fast. "Go for a sleigh ride. How about that?"

"Sounds like fun! What time?"

"Let's say around two. That'll give me time to get the sleigh hitched up." And find one somewhere. Thunder Mountain didn't have one, but surely someone in the area would. A sleigh ride down the snowy Forest Service road sounded like a terrific holiday idea—lots of blankets and maybe some privacy.

"Great. I'll be there. Listen, I have to go. I saw you walk in here and followed you so I could say hi, but my sister's coming into town tonight and—"

"Coming into town? I thought she was living with you."

"Not anymore. I have another woman sharing the house."

"Oh." That didn't help.

"But she's gone for the holidays."

That perked him up fast. "Is that right?"

Amethyst laughed. "You should see your face."

"Sorry. It's just that—"

"I know." Merriment danced in her blue eyes. "We'll talk tomorrow. Maybe we can work something out." Grabbing his arm for balance, she stood on tiptoe and pressed a quick kiss to his mouth. "See you then." She turned and left the store.

He wasn't sure how long he stood there gazing after her while his fevered brain processed her brief but potent kiss and the information about her absent roommate. Okay, so she had to be with her family during the bulk of the holiday, but at some point she'd go home to bed. He'd be with his peeps at Thunder Mountain, but once everyone was sleeping, it wouldn't matter whether he was there or not.

"Sir, can I help you with something?"

He snapped out of his daze and turned toward the hardware store clerk. "Yes, you sure can. For starters I'll take…let me see…seven of these smoke alarms and if you have holiday bags to put them in that would be great." Now that he'd be seeing Amethyst he might as well get her one.

The clerk stacked them into the crook of his arm. "I'll take these up to the counter. Our store bags have a little holly on them."

"That'll do. I also need several outdoor extension cords and whatever LED Christmas lights you have left."

"We moved all the cords and lights to the Christmas decoration section against the far wall."

"Thanks."

"Is there anything else I can help you with?"

"Do you know anyone with a sleigh for rent?"

"You mean like a business that provides sleigh rides? I think one of the guest ranches is offering—"

"No, not the whole ride. I have access to a horse. I just need the sleigh."

"Then I'm afraid I don't know anybody. Sorry."

"No problem. Just thought I'd ask." He wasn't worried. Somebody would have a sleigh he could use. Amethyst was in town and eager to spend time with him. Christmas had just become a whole lot more festive.

2

AMETHYST DROVE TO her parents' house singing at the top of her lungs. She couldn't wait to tell Sapphire that Jake Ramsey was in town. Her sister was the only person on the planet besides Jake who knew about that hot night in Jackson Hole. Talking about it, when it might never happen again, seemed like a mistake. Sapphire had promised to keep it to herself.

Ah, but Amethyst had so hoped it would happen again. She had a gig in Jackson Hole for New Year's Eve and she'd planned to contact him. She'd decided to wait until the last minute, though, in case he was off duty and had a date for New Year's. What they'd shared didn't fit in the category of dating and that made it twenty times more exciting.

But she'd been aware that he could meet someone in Jackson Hole who didn't have big dreams of a recording contract and was willing to work around his shifts at the fire station. Amethyst didn't want to stand in the way of him getting his happily-ever-after even though she wasn't in the market.

He hadn't found anyone, though, or he wouldn't have

asked her to come out to the ranch for a sleigh ride. The boy she'd known in high school and the man she'd enjoyed one scorching night with wasn't a cheater. Far from it. With his sun-bleached hair, green eyes and firefighter physique he was the all-American good guy.

She was a little surprised that some woman in Jackson Hole hadn't snapped him up, but since no one had, she hoped to make use of whatever stolen moments were available while he was here. A sleigh ride into a snowy landscape dotted with pine trees and devoid of people was a good start.

Grady Magee's truck in her parents' driveway told her that he and Sapphire had arrived from Cody. Amethyst was thrilled for her sister, a talented ceramic artist who'd vowed never to become involved with a creative guy again after several debacles. But Grady, whose recycled metal sculptures had taken the art world by storm, had changed her mind.

Coincidentally, Grady and his older brother Liam had also lived at Thunder Mountain for a couple of years while their mom had recovered from a debilitating car accident. Grady had been at the ranch when Jake had lived there, so as she parked behind Grady's truck she decided to immediately mention seeing Jake instead of waiting for a private chat with Sapphire. Come to think of it, Grady and Sapphire might be going to Thunder Mountain for Christmas Eve. Maybe she could tag along.

Dinner with five imaginative people at the table was lively. Clearly, Amethyst's mom, Sheridan High School's art teacher, and her dad, who'd had his own jazz band for years, had welcomed Grady into the fold. Amethyst could see why.

Unlike the other artists Sapphire had dated, he obviously fed her creativity instead of stifling it. Tonight she was 100 percent herself. Her clothes were vibrantly colored and a hand-carved comb held back her auburn hair to show off beaded earrings that dangled to her shoulders. Best of all, every time she looked at Grady her face glowed, so moving to Cody and working in Grady's renovated barn must agree with her.

Conversation flowed so fast that Amethyst didn't have a chance to mention Jake until they were having dessert, chocolate lava cake that was a family favorite.

Grady heaped praise on the dessert. "I could live on this."

"Me, too." Amethyst scooped up another spoonful of cake and syrup. "Before I fall into a sugar-induced coma, though, I wanted to tell you that I met Jake Ramsey in town just before I drove here."

Sapphire's eyes widened. "Oh, really?"

"Yep." Amethyst sent her a warning glance. "We bumped into each other in the hardware store."

"Jake's home for Christmas?" Grady's happy smile was one of his many endearing traits. "I didn't know he was coming back. That's terrific."

"I remember Jake from when you dated him," her mother said. "Nice boy, although he always seemed a little quiet for you."

"He was sort of shy back then. Not as much now." She didn't dare look at Sapphire, who had barely managed to cover a snort of laughter with a cough.

"I haven't seen him in forever," Grady said. "By the time I came back from working that pipeline job in Alaska he'd hired on with the fire department over in Jackson Hole. Did he say if he was still at that job?"

"I believe he is."

"I'll bet firefighting's a good fit for him. We used to tease him about his overdeveloped sense of responsibility. He didn't pull pranks like the rest of us. Anyway, it'll be great to see him. Always liked the guy."

Amethyst could feel her mother's assessing gaze. No doubt she was remembering the gig in Jackson Hole and wondering if there was more to the story than met the eye, especially after Sapphire's "Oh, really?" comment. Jane Ferguson was no fool and when it came to her daughters she seemed to know when a romance was in the making.

But this time her radar was off because there was no romance. Lust, definitely. But romance suggested a soft-focus ending to the story and Amethyst had no interest in that. She was hoping that a talent scout or someone with connections in the music industry would show up at one of her gigs. With luck, that could lead to a recording contract and a move to LA. Marriage and a family didn't fit in with that dream.

After the meal Sapphire offered to clean up the kitchen and recruited Amethyst to help for old times' sake. The minute they were alone she lowered her voice. "So? Did you know about this visit?"

"I didn't, and when I saw him in town I thought that meant he wasn't interested anymore. But you know how I am—can't just let something go. So I followed him into the store to find out for sure if he was deliberately ignoring me."

"And?"

"He's still interested." As she remembered the gleam in his eyes when he'd learned her roommate was gone, she couldn't hold back a grin.

"Then why didn't he contact you?"

"It's Christmas. He has family stuff. I have family stuff."

Sapphire nodded. "Makes sense. But surely you can work something out." She peered at her. "You want to, right?"

"You bet I do. You should have seen him standing there looking all rugged in his sheepskin coat and Stetson. Those green eyes are killer. I was ready to attack him on the spot."

"So what's the plan?"

"For starters he invited me out to the ranch for a sleigh ride tomorrow afternoon."

"You mean a sleigh ride or a *sleigh ride*?" Sapphire wiggled her fingers to make air quotes.

"That's tough to say with so many people around. Besides, it doesn't matter. I let it drop that Arlene is out of town for the holidays."

"She *is*?" Sapphire clapped her hand over her mouth and glanced at the kitchen doorway. "Sorry."

"It's okay. I think Mom already knows something's going on."

"Probably. It's my fault. I didn't expect you to suddenly announce that your red-hot lover boy was in town."

"I wasn't going to. Then I remembered that he and Grady lived at Thunder Mountain at the same time, so I felt obligated to mention it."

"Absolutely. Grady's always thrilled when he gets a chance to connect with some of his foster brothers. Anyway, that's fabulous news about Arlene being gone."

"She's a good roommate. Not as good as you, but we get along and she pays her share of the rent on time."

"I worried that she'd talk you to death. When I worked

with her at the Art Barn co-op she was quite the chatterbox. Sweet, but extremely verbal."

Amethyst smiled. "She is, but I love her work and she's given me a gorgeous watercolor of the Bighorns that I put in my bedroom. Whenever she carries on too long, I suddenly have to record another track for my next album and I scoot upstairs to my studio. Like I said, we get along."

"I'm glad. And she had the good sense to be out of town at a critical moment in your personal life."

"No kidding. Anyway, I need to go home tonight and put clean sheets on the bed and spruce up the place a little."

"Like he'll care. Hey, listen, I know hanging out in a crowd with your studmuffin isn't optimal, but Grady and I are going over to Thunder Mountain tomorrow night for their Christmas Eve celebration if you want to come along. We could—oh, wait, I just remembered something. There's a cat. His name's Ringo. I'll bet Jake's forgotten about your allergies."

"Is Ringo indoor or outdoor?"

"Both. He has a bed in the kitchen. I don't think he gets on the furniture in the house, but still, you don't want to go out there and start sneezing your head off."

"Thanks for the warning. I'll pick up some over-the-counter meds at the drugstore in the morning." She was headed there anyway. If Jake would be spending some late-night quality time at her house, she would be prepared with condoms. "It's one day and one evening with minimal exposure and I don't want to miss out on the fun. I'd love to go, but what about Mom and Dad? I hate to leave them in the lurch."

"They were invited, too, but they think Herb and

Rosie deserve to have Grady and me all to themselves. Mom and Dad claimed us for Christmas Day so it seemed fair to them if we went to the ranch tomorrow night. If you come with us, then they can do their love-bird thing."

"It's cute, isn't it? After all these years they're still nuts about each other."

"Mom pointed that out when I told her I couldn't be with Grady because he was an artist." Sapphire mimicked their mother's voice. "'Your father and I are both artists and we've managed to stumble through twenty-nine years without killing each other.'"

"And so will you and Grady." Amethyst gave her a hug. "You two have something special. The ring he gave you is gorgeous."

"I'm rather fond of it, myself." Sapphire held her hand out in front of her to admire it. "We've tried to set a date but we're both so busy we haven't figured out when."

"Whenever it is, I'll be there, and I want to sing."

"I would love for you to sing but you'll be the maid of honor. Can you do both things? I've never seen that done but if anyone can pull it off you can."

"I've never seen it done, either, but I'll be happy to set a precedent as the first singing maid of honor. I might even sing as I walk down the aisle." She looked at Sapphire. "What do you think?"

"I think it's a fabulous idea. In fact, when you get married, you should be the singing bride. You could sing your vows and turn the whole thing into a musical. Just make sure the groom can sing, too, or it'll be weird."

"Yeah, because having both the bride and groom sing their vows wouldn't be the least bit weird."

Sapphire laughed. "You should do it."

"I definitely would if I planned to get married. But I don't."

"Ever?"

"Probably not. I've watched how it goes with the big names and I'm hoping to be up there with them someday. It's not easy to maintain a high-profile career and a solid marriage."

Sapphire gazed at her as if evaluating the truth of that statement. Finally she nodded. "I guess you're right. You're smart to think that through, because you're going to make it big."

"That's my goal." She crossed her fingers. "But there are no guarantees, either. Even if I get a contract it could be a bumpy ride. It wouldn't be fair to drag some unsuspecting guy along."

"Nope. But I see why you're so excited about hanging out with Jake since he's not looking to settle down, either. You might as well soak up all that yumminess while he's in town."

"My thoughts, exactly."

Six people gathered around the kitchen table at the ranch house that night and, fortunately, Rosie, the woman he'd called *Mom* ever since she'd asked him to the first day, had made plenty of tuna casserole. Jake was on his third helping. Cade had mentioned that several times.

"Leave him alone." Chelsea came to his defense. "He's a growing boy."

"Thanks, Chelsea." Jake hadn't met her until tonight but she was easy to get to know. Her multicolored hair and funky clothes made him smile and he could tell she liked him, too. She worked in marketing and Finn gave her full credit for making his microbrewery a success and for mellowing out his workaholic tendencies. The two of them seemed to have a good thing going.

"He's definitely grown since I last saw him," Finn said. "You put on any more muscle and you'll rip the seams of that shirt, bro. I advise cutting back on the workouts or you'll be shelling out for a new wardrobe."

Cade grinned. "Hey, Finn, you're just jealous because Jake and I are manly men with jobs that increase the diameter of our biceps, while you only have to expend enough energy to put a head on a mug of beer."

"Are you saying I'm out of shape?" Finn propped his elbow on the table and lifted his hand in a challenge. "Arm-wrestle this, pony boy."

Cade left his chair. "My pleasure, suds stud."

"Suds stud?" Chelsea snorted. "I need to remember that one."

Jake wondered if they'd actually arm-wrestle. He wouldn't mind seeing that because he suspected Finn could take Cade. Finn had an air of steely determination, almost an edgy quality, whereas Cade was more easygoing.

"No arm wrestling at the dinner table." Rosie gave them a warning glance. "You know the rules."

"Yeah," Jake said. "Some of us are still eating, here."

"Oh, sorry." Cade sat again. "Wouldn't want to get in the way of that."

Jake smiled before he took another bite. Now that his hunger was mostly satisfied he could savor the taste. "I need to make this at the firehouse. I keep meaning to get the recipe from you." He glanced at Rosie. Short and blonde, with a little extra padding here and there, she was the most beautiful woman he knew. And talk about steely determination. She had it in spades.

"She doesn't use a recipe anymore, son." Herb, the person Jake considered his dad for all intents and purposes, was a wiry guy who could do the work of men half his age.

"Herb's right," she said. "I could make tuna casserole in my sleep. Probably have a time or two. But I'll try to come up with some directions for you. It would be a great firehouse meal. I hadn't thought of that."

"Most of the stuff you made for us would go over great at the firehouse. We look for good food that's not too expensive."

"Which is especially important if they all eat as much as you," Cade said.

"Some eat more." It wasn't true but he'd said it to get a reaction out of Cade.

"They do?"

"Oh, yeah. Once a week a semi backs up to the firehouse to unload our groceries. We make our salad in a wheelbarrow and our spaghetti sauce in a sterilized oil drum. In order to cook the pasta we build a fire under an antique bathtub."

Cade stared at him. "That's amazing."

Jake kept a straight face as long as he could but finally burst out laughing, which set off everybody else.

Cade blew out a breath. "Well, it *could* be true. After watching Jake put away food I was willing to believe it."

"I've always loved seeing my boys eat." Rosie beamed at them. "Who's ready for German chocolate cake?"

Jake left his chair and went over to kiss her cheek. "You made my favorite."

"Of course I did. You haven't been home for Christmas in years. We need to celebrate."

Everybody else seemed happy with the prospect of cake, too, but Jake was touched that she'd remembered how much he loved it. He'd never known his own mother but whenever he imagined what she might have been like, he pictured Rosie. A guy couldn't do any better than having a mom like her.

He helped her dish it and, as they were passing out plates, Herb looked over at Cade. "How come the Christmas lights are out? They were on at dusk but I noticed they're out now. Do we need to check the connections?"

"Nah, the connections are fine." Cade flicked a glance at Jake. "We decided to make a few changes in the morning and since no one will be driving up tonight, Finn and I wanted to save the electricity for now. Everything will be operational for Christmas Eve."

"Okay." Herb seemed unconcerned. "I leave that to you boys. I'm sure it'll look great."

"It will." Cade tucked into his cake.

Jake was glad he'd bought the smoke alarms as gifts and the cords and lights could be slipped into the mix without making a big deal of it. But he had more than Christmas lights on his mind. Before they'd all finished their dessert, he brought up the subject that had been nagging him since making the plan with Amethyst. "I'm looking for a sleigh to rent or borrow. Do any of you know of one?"

Cade paused, his fork halfway to his mouth. "What, now you're Santa Claus? Although if you keep eating like that you'll eventually fit the part."

"I invited a woman for a sleigh ride tomorrow afternoon."

Silence descended on the table as all attention swiveled in his direction.

He hadn't worked through this very well. He'd blame the shock of seeing Amethyst in the hardware store, but now he realized that he couldn't ask for a sleigh without offering more of an explanation.

He cleared his throat. "I made a quick run into town before dinner so I could pick up a few…things."

"It's Christmas." Rosie waved a hand as if to relieve him of giving the details. "We all have secrets. But who's the woman?"

"I ran into her when I was in town. Amethyst Ferguson."

Rosie's gaze sharpened. "You dated her in high school."

"For a while."

"You know she's a professional singer now."

"Yes, I know. Now, about this sleigh, I remember we used to hitch Navarre up to a wagon."

"And a couple of times to a toboggan." Finn exchanged a grin with Cade.

Jake ignored him. "I thought he could probably pull a sleigh."

"He could," Herb said, "but there's the slight problem of not having a sleigh for him to pull."

Cade put down his fork. "You know, that takes cojones, bro, inviting a woman on a sleigh ride when you're not in possession of one. I'm impressed."

"Do you know of anybody who has one?"

"Nope, can't say as I do, but I'm still impressed."

Jake figured there was no point in asking Finn and Chelsea. They didn't live here anymore. In desperation, he turned to Rosie. "Mom, do you know of anyone around here who has a sleigh?"

"Not at the moment, but if you need a sleigh, I'll find you one."

3

LUCK BLESSED JAKE with a clear sky the next morning. If a snowstorm had blown in, which was always possible in December, reconfiguring the lights would have been impossible. As it was the task wasn't simple, especially wearing gloves. Cade and Finn had woven a complex tapestry of dangerous cords and substandard lights.

Cade had apologized for his screw-up and had tried to take the blame, but Finn had insisted on sharing it. He, Cade and Damon were the triumvirate who'd called themselves the Thunder Mountain Brotherhood in the early days of the foster program. Their loyalty to each other ran deep.

Jake respected that. He'd arrived at the ranch later and, although every guy was now considered part of the brotherhood, the bond wasn't the same as the one shared by the first three. When those boys had come to the ranch there had been no tradition, no sense of belonging to something greater. They'd had to create that for themselves.

His buddies at the fire department had a unique connection because they faced life-and-death situations every day, but again, it wasn't the same. Firefighters could choose to quit and sever that connection. The kids who'd been brought to the ranch after the Thunder Mountain Brotherhood had been established could thank Cade, Finn and Damon for creating a positive and lasting identity for all of them. Once a Thunder Mountain brother, always a Thunder Mountain brother.

They'd nearly finished reconfiguring the lights when Rosie walked out onto the porch. She'd pulled a knit cap down over her ears and held her coat closed instead of zipping it, which meant she was making a brief visit. "I think you boys can quit, now. It's not as if the Pope is coming for a visit."

Jake had to laugh. She still called them boys, probably always would.

"But Lexi will be here." Cade arranged the net lights more evenly on a bush. "That's enough motivation for me."

"I'm sure she'll be very impressed. That's more lights than we've ever had on this house. But you need to finish up. I've found Jake a sleigh."

Jake glanced up, a three-pronged plug dangling from his gloved hand. "That's awesome! Where is it?"

"The Emersons have one, but it's too wide to fit in the back of a pickup. Their ranch isn't that far as the crow flies, so it makes more sense to ride over and get it, anyway. It may not be in the best of shape, so I suggest you take Cade or Finn with you."

"We'll all go," Cade said. "It'll be fun."

Jake gazed at her. "What do you mean, not in the best of shape?"

"It hasn't been used in years. They offered to sell it

to me for fifty bucks, so I said fine. I've always wanted a sleigh."

"Um, if it's only fifty bucks it could be falling apart." Jake didn't want to sound ungrateful but he also didn't plan to take Amethyst out in a sleigh that could collapse any minute.

"I asked them and they said it's functional."

"But if they haven't used it in years, how do they know?"

"That's an excellent point." She shivered and stomped her feet. "But I called everyone I could think of and this is the only one I found. If you'd rather not take a chance on it, I'll call them back and say never mind."

"Don't do that," Cade said. "We'll make it work. I've always wanted a sleigh, too."

"Then you'd better finish the lights and get over there. At the very least it'll need to be cleaned up and Amethyst will be here before you know it."

Jake glanced at the angle of the sun. "You're right. Thanks, Mom."

"You're welcome. If the sleigh doesn't work there's a toboggan in the barn. I seem to remember some people hitching a horse to that once upon a time." She winked and went back into the house.

"Nix on the toboggan idea," Cade said. "You can't make out with a woman on a toboggan."

Finn brushed snow off his gloves. "Might be a safer bet than a fifty-buck sleigh."

"That's what I'm thinking." Jake blew out a breath. "It's liable to be a piece of junk."

"Maybe not." Cade came over and clapped him on the shoulder. "Think positive, bro. Maybe it's a gem that's taking up space they want for something else."

"Or maybe the wood's rotted out and the mice have made a nest in the upholstery."

"One way to find out. I have a feeling we can rehabilitate this sleigh." Cade glanced up at the Christmas lights strung everywhere. "Are we done here?"

"You tell me. You're the one trying to impress your ladylove."

Cade nodded. "I think it'll do. If you two put the ladders away I'll start saddling the horses. I'm betting you're both out of practice."

"I can saddle a horse just fine," Jake said. "How about you, O'Roarke?"

"Never lost my touch. But if Gallagher wants to show off his horse whisperer technique, that's fine with me. Saves me the effort."

"Then I'll get started on that." Cade adjusted the fit of his Stetson and headed down to the barn, his boots crunching through the snow.

Finn collapsed one of the extension ladders with a loud clang before turning to Jake. "You know why he's putting so much emphasis on the decorations this year, right?"

"Haven't a clue other than he wants Lexi to think he's a holiday illumination genius."

"It's more than that. Christmas would be the perfect time for Lexi to propose and the more magical the setting, at least in Cade's mind, the more likely she'll pop the question."

"I see. Makes some kind of crazy sense." Jake was well aware of the interesting dynamic between those two. Cade had asked Lexi to marry him a year and a half ago and she'd gently turned him down. So Cade had put her in charge of proposing. "I hope she does it." He collapsed the other ladder and picked it up. "I've never seen a guy so eager to get married."

"I don't know about that. I'm pretty damned excited about marrying Chelsea. Can't wait for April." He picked up his ladder and they both started toward the barn.

"You don't mind the monkey suit and all the fuss?"

"Not really. Chelsea's family is pretty casual, so it won't be stuffy and formal." He looked over at Jake. "Any chance you can come?"

"You know I'd love to. I have to figure out the finances and then see if I can wrangle time off."

"I understand. I don't expect a lot of the guys will make it up to Seattle, but I'm hoping some do."

"At least now I've met Chelsea. She's terrific."

Finn laughed. "You don't have to tell me. Like I said, can't wait for April."

Jake pondered his two brothers and their anticipated marriages as he and Finn put away the ladders and helped Cade finish saddling up the horses. Both guys clearly wanted that kind of permanence. Jake had no such long-range plans.

He was eager for some private time with Amethyst, but he wasn't thinking beyond that. She was perfect for this stage of his life. Before their hot night in Jackson Hole, he'd dated a few women who had been nice but needy.

His job asked a lot of him. He loved the sense of accomplishment it gave him, but he didn't want to be emotionally responsible for someone on top of the demands at work. With Amethyst he didn't have to worry about that. She was focused on her career and didn't need anyone to take care of her.

That included her approach to sex. She asked for what

she wanted more frankly than anyone he'd been with. He loved that about her. This sleigh deal might or might not work out, but tonight after the festivities, he'd—

"Hey, Fireman Jake, you gonna get on that horse or not?"

Cade's voice cut into his libido-driven thoughts. Damn. Caught daydreaming about Amethyst for the second time in two days. He glanced up at Cade, who was mounted on Hematite, the black horse he'd trailered to the ranch summer before last. Finn was already up on Isabeau, Rosie's mare.

Jake, however, stood beside Navarre, Herb's gelding, while staring into space like an idiot. "Yep. Sorry. Just thinking about something." He swung into the saddle.

"More likely some*one*." Cade chuckled as he led the way to the Forest Service road. From there they'd cut across snow-covered open range to the Emerson place. "From what I remember about Amethyst Ferguson, I don't blame you. I wasn't at the high school Christmas concert where she sang 'Santa Baby' but I heard about it."

Finn laughed. "Didn't we all. Were you there, Jake?"

"I was." The road was deserted so they were able to ride three abreast with Cade in the middle. It felt great to be back on a horse again, especially with two of his brothers along. "We'd stopped dating two weeks before that concert. Bad decision on my part."

"*You* broke it off?" Cade glanced at him in disbelief. "I gave you credit for more brains than that."

"Nope. I was young and stupid. I thought she'd looked at another guy in a provocative way. She denied it, but I had that idea stuck in my head and refused to let the whole thing slide. The truth is, she was too hot for me back then."

"But not now, apparently," Finn said.

"No." Jake smiled. "Not now."

Once they hit open country, they picked up the pace a little, but not much since obstacles could be hidden under the snow and the air was still pretty damned cold. Jake wouldn't want to race through this landscape and create a wind chill effect, but a trot was invigorating. He'd picked up a second job at a stable in Jackson Hole because they were willing to work around his shifts, but he wasn't there to ride. Mostly he mucked out stalls and groomed the horses.

As they approached the Emerson ranch, he could see the sleigh sitting out in front of the barn. From here it didn't look too bad. The red paint job had faded and the runners were dull and rusted in spots, but the sleigh might be salvageable.

He glanced at Cade. "What's that luggage rack thing hanging off the back?"

"I guess that's where you put your picnic basket. If you're going for a sleigh ride you might take along hot cocoa, some cookies, maybe."

"I would do that," Finn said. "Sounds cozy."

Jake didn't think the rack looked sturdy enough to hold anything. "So what do you think of the sleigh itself?"

"A new coat of paint and some rust remover and it'll be a beauty," Cade said.

"I wouldn't know," Finn said. "Sleighs are not my area of expertise."

"Not mine, either," Cade said, "but—"

"Hold it." Jake brought Navarre to a halt. "I thought you knew something about sleighs."

Cade shrugged. "What's to know? It's a wagon on skis."

"Yeah, well, that would be the critical difference, wouldn't it? What if those runners are all messed up? What if they somehow malfunction and throw Amethyst into a ditch where she breaks something important like her neck?"

"Settle down, Fireman Jake. I would hope you're not planning to charge down the Forest Service road like you're running the Iditarod."

"Well, no, but—"

"Then we don't have a problem. All you need is a sleigh that will take you at a sedate pace from the ranch to the Forest Service road and from there to a little side lane where you can drink hot cocoa and make out. Am I right?"

Jake sighed. "Yeah."

"Then no worries. That fifty-buck sleigh will fulfill that mission. Let's find Emerson and close the deal."

Twenty minutes later Jake sat on the hard bench seat with the reins in his hands and Navarre hitched to the sleigh. He suspected there was no upholstery because the mice had actually made a nest in it and Emerson had ripped it out before they arrived. The red paint on the seat hadn't faded at all.

The rest was more pink than red. The sleigh looked a lot shabbier up close and he heartily wished he'd suggested a different entertainment to Amethyst, but it was too late, now. Cade had paid the rancher fifty dollars and the sleigh now belonged to Thunder Mountain.

Cade lifted his hand like the leader of a wagon train. "Move 'em out!"

"Oh, for God's sake." But Jake slapped the reins against Navarre's rump and the sleigh went forward, creaking in protest. "Hey, wagon master, this thing is wobbling."

"Of course it's wobbling." Cade seemed unconcerned. "It hasn't had an outing in ten years."

"Ten?" Jake bid goodbye to his fantasy of a romantic sleigh ride. "I didn't hear that part."

"I pinned him down before I gave him the money and he admitted it hadn't been used in ten years, maybe twelve. Actually, I'm guessing it's more like twenty."

The sleigh shuddered as Jake drove it away from the barn. "Why didn't you cancel the sale?"

"Because I really want a sleigh and this one has good bones."

Finn snorted at that. "You know zip about sleighs and you're able to tell this one has good bones?"

"I predict it has broken bones," Jake said. "We'll be lucky to get it back to the ranch in one piece. We might have to leave it by the side of the road like the pioneers had to dump their pianos."

"We can't do that," Finn said. "Littering is against the law in Wyoming. Which means we'd have to figure out how to haul the carcass back to the ranch so we could use it for firewood."

Cade shook his head. "Boys, boys, boys. Where's your faith in the goodness of the universe? Once we get this sleigh back to Thunder Mountain, and we will, then all it needs is a little TLC and it'll shine like a new penny."

"Or disintegrate like an old newspaper," Jake said.

"We're going over this thing with a fine-tooth comb before I put Amethyst in it. It either passes muster or..." He couldn't come up with an alternative.

"Or the toboggan?" Finn asked.

"No, not that." Jake balked at the idea of leading Amethyst down to the barn where she'd find Navarre hitched to a toboggan. "It was one thing when we were kids goofing around but I'd feel dumb using it now."

"See, the sleigh has to work," Cade said. "It'll provide a romantic touch for you and then later on for me and Lexi. This baby could be the final touch, the gesture that puts Lexi over the top."

Jake exchanged a glance with Finn. No doubt they were both thinking the same thing—Lexi needed to put this poor cowboy out of his misery. But Jake could see Lexi's side. Six years ago Cade had left town, apparently spooked by Lexi's urge to get married. When he'd finally showed up ready to tie the knot, Lexi had become her own woman and wasn't so sure she wanted that arrangement anymore.

Jake didn't understand why Cade couldn't simply enjoy the loving relationship and good sex without insisting on a document legalizing the whole thing. But Cade and Finn were both turning thirty next year, so maybe their itch to get hitched made sense. At twenty-seven, Jake hadn't felt it.

Once they were off the ranch property and moving over uneven hillocks of snow, the sleigh rattled and creaked so much that the guys gave up on conversation. They'd made it nearly halfway back when the runners hit something under the snow and the sleigh lurched to one side. It righted itself, but one of the rattles was now a lot worse.

Jake figured it was the luggage rack. "Hey, Cade," he called out. "Can you drop back and see if we're about to lose a piece of this contraption?"

"Sure." He pulled Hematite to a stop and waited while Jake passed him. Then he dropped in behind the sleigh. "Yeah, I see a few screws missing on the rack. Matter of fact, the whole thing could go, now that I look at the way it's leaning. You'd better hold up so we can evaluate the situation."

"But it's got good bones, right, Gallagher?" Finn wheeled Isabeau around and rode to the back of the sleigh. "Crap, that doesn't look good."

Jake climbed down and trudged through the snow to where his brothers had dismounted to assess the damage. The metal rack dangled, held in place by a couple of screws. The rest were AWOL. "We need to take it off before it falls off."

"With what?" Cade looked at him. "You packing a screwdriver?"

"No. Anybody got a penny? I don't like carrying change so I don't."

"I'm the same about change in my pockets," Finn said. "Bugs me."

Cade shrugged. "I don't have any, either. Maybe we should just keep going and let it fall. It's not like we won't hear it."

"You don't want to do that." Finn pointed to a crack in the wood next to one of the screws. "There's a lot of stress being put on the section where the remaining screws are. Once it goes, it could take a chunk of this back section with it. Then this thing will look like hell."

"Then I have a suggestion." Jake thought the sleigh already looked like hell but saying it wouldn't change anything. "If one of you gets in the sleigh with me, you can lean over the back and hold on to it. The other one can lead the extra horse."

"I'll hold the rack," Cade said. "But, Finn, you need to switch horses. Hematite isn't fond of being behind another horse."

"Then I'll hold the rack and you lead Isabeau," Finn said. "She's a sweetheart who doesn't mind being last." He handed the mare's reins to Cade.

"No, *I'll* hold the rack while Finn drives," Jake said. "If I hadn't invited a woman for a sleigh ride before I had the damn sleigh, we wouldn't be doing any of this."

"But where's the fun in that?" Cade grinned at him. "We're making us some memories right here."

"I guarantee I won't be forgetting this anytime soon." Jake climbed into the bench seat and leaned over to grasp the metal rack. "Better take it slow, O'Roarke. This isn't a real stable position I have, here."

Cade chuckled. "No, but it sure is a photo op. Wish I'd brought my phone so I could take a picture of you riding in that sleigh ass backward."

"Thank God for small favors. Knowing you, you'd put it on the internet."

"Yeah, I would."

Jake listened to the sleigh rattle along. It wasn't as noisy now because he was holding the rack and they were going slower. "Say, Cade, when are Damon and Phil due at the ranch?"

"They were hoping to hit town late this morning and stop by around lunchtime. They could be there now."

"That would be great."

"They'll be tired," Finn said. "And Phil's less than a month away from her due date, which is why they drove to Florida. Just in case you were hoping they could do a quick fix."

"I don't expect that, but they could give me their opinion on whether this thing is roadworthy before Amethyst arrives. How are we doing on time?"

"I'd estimate it's about one fifteen," Cade said. "Give or take."

"Yikes. I hope Amethyst's not early."

But of course she was. As Finn drove the sleigh into the open area in front of the barn, Amethyst climbed out of her yellow SUV. She took one look at Jake's position in the sleigh and started laughing. Terrific. His rep was ruined. Might as well hitch up the toboggan.

4

AMETHYST WOULD RECOGNIZE those buns anywhere. She'd admired them when Jake was seventeen and they'd become even more worthy of a good ogle since then. But the sleigh…oh, my God. She'd assumed when he'd invited her that Thunder Mountain Ranch had a sleigh, probably painted hunter green and brown, the colors of Thunder Mountain Academy.

Apparently, Jake had issued his invitation prematurely. His cheeks were tinged pink as he walked toward her and she doubted the cold was to blame. But, damn, he was gorgeous. Who cared what the sleigh looked like when she could feast her eyes on a muscled cowboy with soulful green eyes and a sculpted mouth that could kiss like nobody's business?

"I have to apologize," he said.

"No, you don't. That entrance was worth the trip out here."

"Yeah, I'll bet. I'm surprised you didn't whip out your phone."

"Wish I had." She wouldn't have minded a permanent

record of Jake's sexy butt. But she'd been too mesmerized to think of it.

"Look, obviously we don't have a working sleigh, so I'm afraid—"

"Don't be hasty, Fireman Jake!" Cade hurried over. "Hey, Amethyst. Good to see you." He touched the brim of his hat.

"Good to see you, too, Cade. I don't think we've run into each other since the last time I saw you at Rangeland Roasters having coffee with Lexi."

"I know. Sheridan's a small town, but you can go months without meeting up with folks who live here."

"And I'm on the road a lot."

"Yeah, I know! Love your music. Lexi and I listen to you all the time. Anyway, I don't want you two to give up on the sleigh ride just yet. Finn's unhitching Navarre so we can get to work on the chassis."

Jake shook his head. "It's no use, Gallagher. It might be salvageable but it'll take days."

"I'm not promising it'll look brand new in five minutes, but Damon and Phil are here and they never go anywhere without tools. It's possible with their help we can clean this baby up, tighten a few screws and she'll be good enough for a little ride down the Forest Service road. Have you had lunch, Amethyst? Rosie always has plenty to eat and you could relax inside while we work our magic."

"Yes, I've had lunch. And, really, we can skip the sleigh ride. I don't want anyone to go to a lot of trouble on Christmas Eve day."

"Me, either," Jake said. "Maybe Amethyst and I could just—"

"Jake, I'm telling you, it won't take much. I'm sure

Mom filled in Damon and Phil over lunch. They'd probably be insulted if we *didn't* ask them."

"I doubt it," Jake said. "They just got back from Florida, dude. And Phil's not in any shape to help."

"All the more reason not to bother them," Amethyst said. "Jake can give me a tour of the place. I've heard so much about it over the years but I've never visited."

"Hey, Jake Ramsey!" Damon's deep voice carried through the crisp air as he strode toward them. "What's this I hear about a fixer-upper sleigh?"

"Hey, Damon." Jake went to meet him. "Just my latest idiotic move."

Amethyst was touched by their warm embrace. She'd always had a soft spot in her heart for the Thunder Mountain boys. Most of them had some tragedy in their background and Jake was no exception. When they were dating she'd learned that his mom had died when he was a toddler and his father had turned into an abusive alcoholic. Jake used to spend his nights wherever he could get away from the beatings, sometimes at the home of a friend and sometimes hidden in the storeroom of Scruffy's Bar.

Jake didn't trust easily. She'd learned that when he'd broken up with her over a stupid misunderstanding. He'd never quite believed that she cared about him and he still might not. But at least they had a sexual connection that made them both happy.

She watched as Jake and Damon walked over to the sleigh. They were both laughing as Damon examined it from all angles. She turned to Cade. "I love your can-do attitude but, seriously, let's forget about the sleigh ride, okay? It was a cute idea but I can live without it."

"But that would mean giving up," Cade said. "Besides, Damon likes to show off his manly carpentry skills."

"That may be true but—"

"In these situations, it's best to sit back and let the Thunder Mountain Brotherhood do its thing."

She let out a breath. "Okay, I'll try."

Damon and Jake continued to joke around as they walked back over to where she stood with Cade.

"Damon's convinced me we need to give this sleigh a chance," Jake said. "So I'm prepared to work with him on it if you're willing to allow us a little time."

"Sure, why not? What do you want me to do?"

"I'm not going to put you to work, if that's what you're thinking. While Damon's assessing the job, let's go inside and see Rosie. I know you've had lunch but she'll have a pot of coffee going and I happen to know there's some German chocolate cake left over from last night."

"That sounds great." Amethyst hadn't known what to expect from this afternoon but she hadn't planned on much alone time with Jake, anyway. She'd popped an antihistamine before driving out here in case she ended up in the same space with Ringo the cat.

"I'll go in with you," Cade said. "I'm starving and I can only imagine your hunger pangs, Fireman Jake. From what I've seen, you need fuel and plenty of it. I'd hate to see you grow weak from lack of food."

"So you all missed lunch?" Amethyst was overwhelmed by the group effort to provide her with a sleigh ride.

"Yeah, but Finn's probably in there wolfing down a sandwich by now," Cade said. "Sad to say, Jake and I haven't taken any sustenance since breakfast."

"Then, by all means, let's all go in so you guys can get fed."

Shortly thereafter Amethyst was seated at Rosie's kitchen table with a mug of coffee and a slice of cake. Jake and Cade each had hefty sandwiches to go with their coffee. Finn had already left to help Damon, but his fiancée Chelsea was there along with Philomena, Damon's redheaded and exceedingly pregnant wife. Ringo, a gray tabby, was curled up in a bed in the corner, but the antihistamine was working so Amethyst was fine.

Jake paused between bites to address his foster mom, who'd joined them with coffee and cake. "Where's Dad?"

"In town, Christmas shopping."

"He still waits until the last minute?"

Rosie laughed. "He claims that's when he feels the Christmas spirit, when everyone in town is racing the clock."

"What he feels is frantic desperation," Cade said. "You couldn't pay me to be in town today."

Jake laughed. "How does two grand sound?"

"Okay, I'd do it for that."

"Case closed." Jake finished his sandwich and pushed back his chair. "Mom, that was wonderful." He glanced over at Amethyst. "Will you be okay for a little while? This shouldn't take long."

"Are you kidding? You're leaving me with interesting women and German chocolate cake. I'll be more than fine." Amethyst discovered she liked seeing him in this setting, surrounded by his foster family. He seemed emotionally stronger and more confident here. She wished he'd brought her to the ranch when they'd been dating but there'd been no reason.

Cade went with him, which left Rosie, Chelsea and Phil at the table with Amethyst.

She knew a little about Phil, who'd worked as a contractor in Sheridan for several years before meeting and falling in love with Damon. But Chelsea was a complete stranger so Amethyst started the conversation by asking about her work and how she'd happened to meet Finn. Turned out they'd been in line for coffee and had started up a conversation that had led to a business relationship and eventually love.

"Chelsea's been so good for him," Rosie said. "He's still very focused on his work, but he's not as driven as he used to be."

"The more I'm around the Thunder Mountain guys," Phil said, "the more I've noticed that most of them have a strong urge to succeed. Considering the crummy background they had, it's not surprising. Damon's mellowing out, finally, which is good. I want him to be able to relax enough to enjoy his kid."

Amethyst had abandoned the idea of having children when she'd decided on her career path, but she was curious all the same. "How's motherhood so far?"

"Disconcerting." Phil laid a hand over her big belly. "Normally, I work side by side with Damon on our renovation jobs, but in the last month that's been increasingly difficult. Life should be easier when she's born. I plan to pack her along on jobs, at least until she's mobile. Then I might need day care."

"So you're having a girl?" Amethyst asked.

"Oh, yeah, and I'm thrilled about that."

"So am I." Rosie sipped her coffee. "This ranch is loaded with testosterone, in case you hadn't noticed."

Amethyst smiled. "I've noticed, but I'm not complaining. I grew up with a sister."

Rosie's gaze warmed. "How's Sapphire doing? From a sister's perspective, I mean. Grady says everything's going well, but I had a little something to do with her decision to move to Cody and I dearly hope it's working out."

"It definitely is. You'll see for yourself tonight when they come to your Christmas Eve party."

"Are you coming?" Chelsea asked.

"Or more to the point," Phil said, "are you staying? You're here for this major-deal sleigh ride, so unless you have plans you might as well stay for the rest of the evening."

Amethyst was struck by the logic of it. She'd considered coming over later with Grady and Sapphire but that might not make any sense. She glanced at the kitchen clock. If the sleigh was cleaned up and ready before three, she'd be amazed. And dusk came early in December.

Then she looked down at her simple top and jeans. "I'm not dressed for a Christmas Eve gala."

Rosie laughed. "Honey, you're at Thunder Mountain Ranch. Around here we pay more attention to the people than the clothes they're wearing. Besides, you look very nice."

"All righty, then. I'd love to stay."

"Great!" Chelsea smiled at her. "Now that we have that settled, I'm dying to ask about your career. I understand you're a professional singer."

"I'm working at it. So far my gigs have all been in Wyoming and that's where I get the bulk of my music sales, too."

Chelsea's expression was animated. "Have you sent out demos?"

"I have, but no takers yet from the studios. I hoping for a big break eventually, but in the meantime I'm giving private voice lessons, mostly to kids. That's fun."

"I'll bet it would be," Phil said. "I love hearing little kids sing. Warms my heart."

"Mine, too." Amethyst smiled as she thought about Jenny, her favorite. "I have one little eight-year-old who has real promise. Cute as a button and that girl can sing. I can't wait to see what happens with her. Then there's a little guy who's only five but he really belts out those tunes. It's adorable. He could go places."

"I wonder if singing is like acting," Chelsea said. "You have to actually be in LA or New York in order to make something happen. Or Nashville if you're doing country."

"Maybe. I'm pop, not country, so it would be New York or LA for me." Amethyst always grew uneasy when this subject came up. "And I would go if I had some interest from one of the major studios. You know, a serious nibble. Moving to the city without that seems pretty darned risky. Sure, I could wait tables, but those are pricey places to live. I'd go through my savings in no time. At least here the cost of living is lower so I can support myself between the gigs I pick up and the private lessons."

"It *is* risky." Rosie got up to bring them all more coffee. "I was worried sick about Finn when he took off for Seattle to open a microbrewery. He didn't know a soul, but he'd researched the market and was convinced that was the best place to be." She gave Chelsea a fond look. "Then he met the right woman and it all worked out."

"He was really lucky," Amethyst said.

"So was I." Chelsea leaned back in her chair. "I'm grateful that he took that risk. I can't imagine my life without him."

"Finn's not the only one who's done that kind of thing," Rosie said. "One of my boys is out in LA right this minute trying to make it as an actor."

"Oh, yeah?" Phil looked over at her. "Who's that?"

"Matt Forrest."

"I remember him from high school!" Amethyst put down her mug and stared at Rosie. "He was a skinny kid one year behind me."

"Well, he's not skinny anymore," Rosie said. "Got a growth spurt, filled out, took some acting classes at the community college. Then he headed to LA. He's been there almost three years now. Like you'd expect, he's had to wait tables and take jobs making commercials. He had one bit part in a small-budget movie and I guess somebody from a major studio liked what they saw. The other day he called to say he was up for something much bigger."

"Wow, I hope he gets it. He seemed like a nice guy the few times I was around him." Amethyst cradled her mug in both hands as she imagined buying a one-way plane ticket to LA or New York and toughing it out for three years. She just didn't like the odds. "What I'm hoping is that I'll have some talent scouts in the audience one of these times. Entertainment folks often vacation in Wyoming."

"They do," Phil said. "They even buy homes here. Damon and I have done some renovations for some Hollywood types. Behind-the-camera people, not anyone you'd recognize."

"I've had some celebrity spottings in Seattle," Chelsea said. "It's always a thrill."

After that the conversation turned to actors, movies and which ones might win an Oscar, but Amethyst kept thinking about Matt Forrest. Maybe she was making a big mistake by not relocating to LA and hiring an agent. New York seemed like a different country to her, but LA wasn't *that* far from Wyoming.

"Sleigh's ready!" Cade came into the kitchen grinning. "Come on down!"

Amethyst glanced at him. "So where's Jake?"

"He's still fiddling with it, but Damon has declared it operational and Finn's hitching up Navarre."

"Then let's go take a look." Phil groaned as she rose from her chair. "At times like this I wish the stork brought the kid, after all."

Cade helped her on with her coat. "Aw, Phil, last I heard you loved being pregnant."

"That was last month. I've revised my opinion."

Once they were all bundled up, they walked down to the barn. Finn was hitching a brown horse to a sleigh that Amethyst thought didn't look half-bad. The rack Jake had been holding in place when they'd pulled in was gone and the dust and grime had been wiped away. If the sleigh didn't exactly sparkle, at least it looked clean.

Blankets had been piled onto the seat and allowed to spill over the edges, which covered some of the more faded parts of the chassis. Damon and Jake crouched near the back, each with a screwdriver as they tightened the struts attached to the runners.

Damon stood as they approached. "Your chariot awaits, milady."

"It's a huge improvement." She smiled at him. "Thank you for all the hard work."

"It didn't take much to make it serviceable. Making it pretty will require a lot longer."

"But we'll do it," Cade said. "Before we're finished you won't recognize this sleigh."

"We could put the Academy students to work on it," Rosie said. "That's if Damon or Phil would be willing to supervise."

"What a brilliant idea!" Phil beamed at her. "I volunteer to supervise. I'm going crazy sitting at home while Damon does all the fun stuff."

Damon rolled his eyes. "Yeah, she is. Great suggestion, Rosie." Then he turned back to the sleigh. "Your passenger has arrived, Ramsey. The runners are fine for now."

"Just making sure of that. Don't want us taking a header into a snowbank."

"You won't if you drive slow and easy."

Cade laughed. "You don't have to worry about it. Enter the word *cautious* into your browser and Fireman Jake will be staring back at you."

"Okay, okay. I get the point." Jake stood and walked over to Damon. "Here's your screwdriver, bro. Thanks for stepping in." Then he turned to Amethyst. "Ready?"

"You bet." She let him hand her into the sleigh while everyone stood around watching. She had the oddest feeling, as if they were a newly married couple leaving on their honeymoon. To her great surprise, she wasn't horrified by the image.

When he walked around the sleigh, climbed in next to her and took the reins, the feeling grew stronger. This was only a sleigh ride, she reminded herself. They'd be back in an hour or so.

"Have fun!" Rosie called out as Jake slapped the reins against the horse's rump and the sleigh began to move.

"We will!" Amethyst turned and waved, and they all waved back. She waited until they'd gone through the pasture gate and were far enough away that no one could hear before she spoke. Even then she kept her voice down. "Just so you know, we can't have sex on this sleigh ride."

He chuckled. "Is that so?" He kept his eyes on the path ahead. "Why not?"

She forced herself to resist that sexy chuckle. And the way his gloved hands on the reins reminded her of how he'd touched her last summer. "I'm not going right home afterward. Phil suggested I stay for the Christmas Eve celebration."

"That's great, but what does it have to do with anything?"

"If we have sex, I'll get all rumpled and kissed-looking. I'll have no way to repair the damage. When I walk back into the ranch house, everyone in your family will know what we've been doing."

"And you'd be embarrassed. I get that."

She sighed in relief. "Good. Because otherwise I'd want to."

"That's nice to hear."

"But I like the sleigh ride. I've never had one before. Cozy."

"Mmm."

"Thank you for going to so much trouble."

"You're welcome." He drove the sleigh in silence for a little while. "What if I told you we could have sex and you wouldn't end up all 'rumpled and kissed-looking'? Would you want to?"

"How could you manage that?" Her body began to hum.

"Trust me when I say I could. I learned early how to cover my tracks."

Her heartbeat accelerated. "I see."

"Kissing is fantastic, especially with you, but it's not a requirement for what I have in mind."

"I suppose not." Moisture dampened her panties.

"Well?" He glanced at her. Although his hat cast a shadow over his green eyes, the heat shimmering there was unmistakable.

She swallowed. "I think I'd be a fool to say no."

5

JAKE HAD BEEN hard as an ax handle ever since they'd gone through the pasture gate and escaped the watchful eyes of his family. He hadn't expected Amethyst to lay down a no-sex rule, but once she'd explained her reasons, he'd understood. Then he'd set to work figuring a way around the issue.

Not kissing her as a warm-up would seem strange, but he'd forgo that if it meant he'd be able to make the connection his body had ached for since she'd driven away from Jackson Hole. He'd considered asking someone else out. After all, he hadn't known whether he'd ever have that experience again with Amethyst, which made celibacy ridiculous.

But that red-hot memory had seared itself into his brain and he couldn't imagine taking another woman to bed until he knew for sure Amethyst was lost to him. Turned out she wasn't the least bit lost. She was right beside him and as eager for him as he was for her.

Fortunately smoke alarms hadn't been the only thing he'd picked up during his quick trip to town. After discovering that she was willing to make time for him, he'd added a quick trip to the drugstore. He'd tucked a condom in his jeans' pocket this morning to make sure he didn't forget.

As the sleigh's runners whispered over the ice and snow on the Forest Service road, he listened for any signs that the struts weren't holding. So far, so good.

But one question nagged him and he finally had to ask it. "Have you dated anybody since Jackson Hole? If you have, that's fine. It's been six months and I can't expect you to—"

"Nobody, Jake."

Music to his ears. "Me, either. Please don't think I'm trying to turn this into a commitment because we were both clear on that."

"There's no commitment," she said softly. "But, face it, that night was crazy. I couldn't imagine duplicating that with anyone else. So I didn't bother looking around."

"Neither did I."

"But you're gorgeous and you must have women who—"

"First of all, thanks, and second of all, none of them interested me. I know we're not making any promises, but compared to you, everyone else is boring."

She laughed. "Every woman wants to hear that at least once in her life! I appreciate the sentiment more than you know. But, Jake, what if even we can't duplicate what we had in Jackson Hole? What if that was a special time that will never happen again?"

"I don't believe that."

"And I certainly don't want to, but think back to August."

"I do. All the time."

"We hadn't seen each other in years and suddenly

we're fulfilling all of these fantasies. Maybe that's the best it'll ever be."

"You're depressing the hell out of me, Amethyst. No wonder some of your love songs are so sad."

She laughed again. "I just wonder if we should be realistic about this."

"You go ahead and be realistic. At the moment my cock aches so much that I don't care whether the sex is good or bad. I just want to have it."

"Wow, okay. I'm fairly desperate myself."

"You are?" He took heart from that. "Then help me look for a road that goes off to the right. It goes down a ways and then there's a wide spot where I can turn the sleigh around. We don't want to get stuck."

"You're taking me to one of your old make-out spots, aren't you?"

"Yes."

"You never brought me out here." She sounded miffed about it.

"It was too far from your house. Besides, you always made me nuts. I was afraid if I brought you to some secluded place like this I'd lose control."

"But I wanted you to! Jake, you were my choice, the one I wanted to give my virginity to."

That stunned him. "I was?" His deeply imbedded cautious streak had drawbacks, and this would be one of them. "So who…"

"Not Eddie, the one you thought I was making eyes at. I never dated him, never wanted to. We were joking around. I heard from him a few months ago. He's come out."

"He's gay?"

"A lot of us suspected it."

"Not me." And he'd caused her grief because he'd been a bonehead. "I'm sorry, Amethyst."

"It worked out for the best. If we'd kept dating that could have changed—hey, is that your turnoff?" She pointed to a narrow road leading into the woods.

"That's it." He pulled Navarre to a stop and gazed at the snowbank blocking the road. Looked like a plow had come through recently. "Damn."

She turned to him, her blue eyes sparkling. Today she'd worn a blue knit cap that matched her eyes. "What's wrong with right here?"

"On the main road?"

Reaching over, she cupped his face in her gloved hands. "I love it when you get that shocked look in your eyes. Makes me want to do outrageous things with you."

"Oh." His breathing rate picked up and his cock pressed painfully against his fly. He remembered her seductive gaze and how effectively it could erase all his misgivings.

"No one is out here but us." She stroked her thumbs over his cheeks as her eyes glowed with excitement. "Tell me what to do."

He barely had enough air to speak. "Take off everything from the waist down."

"Okay."

The air was perfectly still, not a breeze or a bird chirping or the rumble of an approaching vehicle. The only sound was the soft rustle of Amethyst removing her clothes. Golden light filtering through the trees told him sunset was approaching.

Before he could stop himself he'd pulled off his gloves and reached beneath the blankets. When he encountered warm, silky skin, he groaned. "Hold still. Let me…"

Her breath caught. "Oh, Jake."

"It's been so long." He slipped his hand between her thighs, his gaze locked with hers. "So long since I've touched you."

"I know."

"So long since I've made you come." Sliding his fingers deep, he began stroking her in the sensuous rhythm he'd learned that she needed.

With a soft moan she lifted her hips, inviting him deeper as heat blazed in her eyes. "I've...missed you."

"I'm here." He coaxed her higher and gloried in the flush on her cheeks and the way her lips parted in anticipation of...yes!

She surrendered with a soft cry of release, her body trembling and her breath coming in short gasps.

He wanted to kiss her more than he wanted to breathe, but he'd promised not to muss her, so he slowly eased away. Desire rushed through him with such force that his next movements were clumsy. Somehow he retrieved the condom from his jeans before letting them fall to the floor of the sleigh. Once his cock was free he had trouble tearing the foil on the condom.

A soft murmur sounded next to his ear. "Can I help?"

"No." He felt her body heat. Then her fingers brushed his thigh. *"Don't."*

"But I want—"

"Don't touch me, Amethyst. I'll go up in flames."

"I love hearing you come, Jake."

"And I'm really close." He wondered if he'd ever tell her she was the only woman who made him react with such intensity. He rolled on the condom. "I should..." He paused to gulp in air. "I should sit in the middle."

"Good idea." She moved to the far edge of the bench seat to make room for him.

He slid over. "Now."

"Can I touch you?"

His laughter was strained. "Gonna have to."

"We'll never forget this." She turned to face him and put one hand on his shoulder.

"I wouldn't want to."

Her eyes simmered with passion as she slid one bare leg over his thigh. "Me, either."

He shuddered. "I would love to kiss you."

"I would love to kiss you, too." She gripped his shoulders and balanced on her knees. "But I like knowing this will be our secret."

"Yeah."

"Grab hold of my hips."

He closed his eyes and savored the curved perfection of her body. "My fingertips remember you."

"My body remembers your fingertips." Her voice was husky. "Now show me the way to my favorite place."

He opened his eyes so he could see the response in hers. Carefully he guided her until she was poised above his waiting cock. Then he urged her downward until the tip made contact. Her pupils widened and a murmur of pleasure escaped her lips.

His heart beat like a wild thing. "You're in charge."

Looking into his eyes, she began a slow descent. She swallowed. "We need to do this more often."

He nodded. Forming words at a moment like this was beyond him. He concentrated on holding back when all he wanted to do was thrust upward and claim his release. That wouldn't be fair. She'd agreed to this crazy stunt and she deserved all the enjoyment he could give her.

By the time they were locked together she was panting. Then he felt a ripple over his cock. Thank God. She wasn't far behind him.

"This won't take long." Her breathy words were followed by a groan. "Not long at all." And she began to ride him, slowly at first and then faster.

Because he had his hands full of Amethyst, he couldn't control the blankets. They slid to the floor of the sleigh. He didn't care. The friction she was creating between them was generating enough heat that he wouldn't be surprised if the snow surrounding them melted away.

"I'm coming. I'm coming, Jake." She gasped for breath.

"I know." He felt her tremors and abandoned himself to the needs pounding through his body. "Amethyst... *Amethyst.*" His spasms blended with hers. Oh, yes, he remembered this, too, the incredible feeling of sharing a climax with her. Something magical happened in that moment, something he'd never had with another woman. For a short space of time, they became one.

At least he thought they did. He'd never asked her about it because they'd agreed on the parameters. They'd enjoy a fun sexual relationship whenever it was convenient. Magic didn't figure into it. A meeting of souls didn't figure into it, either. She'd probably laugh if he started talking that kind of nonsense.

Eventually they both caught their breath and could focus well enough to look at each other. They both smiled.

"So good," he murmured.

Her gaze was soft. "Better than I remember."

"And that's saying something." He sighed. "Normally

I'd kiss you right now," he said. "But there's nothing normal about this situation."

"No, but it was fun."

"And satisfying."

"Very." She moved away from him with considerate delicacy. "Over to you. The next part is your department."

"I thought of that. All I need is my jeans, if you'd be willing to find them on the floor."

"Sure." She reached down and picked them up. "Better get dressed quick and wrap up in a blanket before the heat wears off."

"Yes, do that." He located the bandanna in his back pocket and used it to take care of the condom. "I don't want you getting chilled on Christmas Eve."

"And thanks to you I won't be frustrated." She wiggled into her jeans. "I wondered if I'd spend the evening in a constant state of arousal. But I should be okay."

"I'm not sure I will be. This might have only whetted my appetite for you."

She paused to gaze at him. "Are you saying we'll be worse off than we were before?"

"That might not be possible." He put on his jeans. "I was a desperate man."

"In a sleigh with a desperate woman."

"Who announced we couldn't have sex!"

She laughed. "Obviously, I wasn't thinking creatively. In my experience a great round of sex leaves the participants looking pretty ragged."

He finished putting on his boots and glanced over at her. "For the record, you look fantastic."

"Yes, but can you tell I've had sex?"

"I can, but I have inside intel."

"Pretend you didn't. Do you think you'd know?"

"Your cheeks are very pink."

"It's cold outside."

"And your eyes sparkle."

"It's Christmas Eve. My eyes always sparkle on Christmas Eve. I love this time of year."

"Me, too." He arranged the blankets over them, put on his gloves and repositioned his hat, which had stayed on through the entire incident. "I'm loving it more every minute."

"So what if I hadn't followed you into the hardware store? Would you have called or texted?"

Taking hold of the reins, he executed a maneuver that wasn't particularly elegant but got them headed back to the ranch. "Honestly, no. On the drive into town I'd made up my mind not to contact you. Then I turned around and there you were."

"Then let's make a bargain. If either of us is going to be in the other person's area, we'll send a text even if we're worried about interrupting something. If so, the one being contacted can always say it's a bad time."

"You're right. But we need complete honesty. If you've lost interest or found someone else, I want to know that. I don't want to hear that it's a bad time if it'll never be a good time again."

Reaching under the blanket, she squeezed his thigh. "I can't imagine losing interest."

"I can't, either, especially when you put your hands on me."

"That bothers you?"

"You have no idea. But I only brought one condom." She sighed. "Which is fine because they'll be expecting us back. But after the party's over, are you coming to my place?"

"I'd like that."

"You're invited. Maybe then we can finally have noisy sex."

That made him laugh. "You've been craving more noise?"

"Sort of. In the hotel room we had to be considerate of the people in the adjoining rooms. Out here we couldn't be yelling because sound carries and someone might call the sheriff."

"That can happen when you're making out in the boonies." He could think of one embarrassing incident when he'd been attending community college and had brought a woman out here. She'd been vocal and he'd almost been arrested.

"Yes, I know."

"Mmm." He didn't want to think of her having sex in the woods with someone else. Yet he'd had sex in the woods with someone else. They were both adults with a history, so what was his problem?

"That was an interesting sound."

"Was it?"

"If I didn't know better, I'd say it was the sound a man makes when he's jealous."

He had to chew on that for a moment. "Being jealous of someone you're not seeing anymore would be dumb, but I…" Gazing at her, he felt a tug at his heart that had nothing to do with excellent sex and everything to do with stronger, deeper emotions he wasn't prepared to discuss.

But that didn't mean he couldn't ask for what he needed to see if she'd go along with it. "Last summer we agreed that we'd meet up when we could, no obligations, which left us free to date—or, more accurately, have sex with…someone else in the meantime."

"True."

"Turns out I'm not happy with that idea. I actually hate it. But I didn't realize that until now." He took a deep breath. "So I propose a new arrangement. If it doesn't suit you, I need to know."

She nodded, although she seemed wary. "Fair enough."

"My plan is to see each other more often and agree not to have sex with anyone else unless we're ready to end the relationship, loose though it may be."

"Then we'd make definite plans to be together?"

"Would that bother you?"

"If you're asking if the prospect of more time with you and more regular sex would bother me, the answer is no. If you're asking if a more formal arrangement bothers me, the answer is yes. I realize I'm contradicting myself."

He completely understood her reluctance. "I'm not working up to marriage, Amethyst. I know your plans don't lead in that direction. But going six months without holding you in my arms is too damned long."

"I've missed you, too." She smiled. "FYI, I have a gig in Jackson Hole for New Year's."

"You do? That's great! Why didn't you let me know when you booked it?"

"I didn't want to interfere if you'd found someone special you wanted to take out for New Year's Eve."

"I have and she's you. I'll be there for that show and afterward we'll celebrate."

"But no strings."

"Absolutely no strings except one. No getting naked with someone else for now."

"I don't want to, anyway."

He let out a sigh of relief. "Good." Spending more time with her would strengthen those feelings that he couldn't talk about. Logically only a fool would want to be with someone who would ultimately leave, but when it came to Amethyst, logic went out the window.

6

AMETHYST HELPED JAKE carry the blankets into the tack room and while he unhitched Navarre she folded and stacked them on an empty shelf. Her body still hummed from her amazing orgasms and she looked forward to many more in the future.

Although Jake would have to leave after Christmas, she'd see him again on New Year's. Getting together on Valentine's Day seemed like a fine idea and she'd be sure to suggest it. Life had suddenly become a lot more interesting.

Being with Jake had always seemed right, even at seventeen. But if she'd been granted her wish and he'd been her first, life could have turned out very differently for both of them. At that age she hadn't been sure a professional career was for her. A college music professor she'd idolized had told her she had the talent to make it, but if she'd been madly in love with Jake at the time, she might not have listened.

The barn door opened, letting in a blast of cold air. "I'll give him a quick rubdown in his stall," Jake called out as he came into the barn leading Navarre.

"Go on down there. Let me get the door." She hurried past him and pulled it closed.

"Thanks. Could you please grab the grooming caddy? It's that plastic thing with all brushes and currycombs in it."

"Will do." She wasn't an expert on horses, but she recognized what he was talking about and took it down from a shelf. She'd always liked the earthy smell of barns and the sounds of horses moving around in their stalls. She and Sapphire had done some riding as kids but they hadn't kept it up as adults.

Jake had left Navarre's stall door open so she walked right in. As the horse munched on a flake of hay, Jake stroked his glossy brown neck and murmured to him.

"I hope you're telling him how much we appreciate him pulling the sleigh," Amethyst said.

"I am." Jake glanced up and smiled. "Navarre was my favorite when I lived here."

"He's been around that long?"

"Sure has. He and Isabeau were about eight when I came to the ranch, so they must be twenty-five or six by now."

"Wow, should we have hitched him to the sleigh at his age?"

"Absolutely. Some horses live to be forty. He's still in his prime."

"Now that you mention it, he doesn't look old at all. I love that he and Isabeau are named after the characters in *Ladyhawke*. Do you know who came up with that?"

"I'm pretty sure Mom and Dad named them. They're both romantics at heart."

"That's not hard to believe." She held up the tote. "Where do you want the caddy?"

"You can put it down right there. I'll come get what I need." He placed his hand on Navarre's rump as he walked around him and came toward her.

She loved Jake's hands—so strong and yet so tender. Having exclusive access to him and his talented hands in her hotel room last summer had been a dream come true. He'd had a knack for caressing a woman when he was seventeen, which had been one of many reasons she'd wanted him to be her first lover. Since then he'd turned his natural talent into an art form.

When she looked up at him, she had a feeling his thoughts weren't far from hers. The brim of his hat shadowed his eyes, but that didn't diminish the force of his gaze.

He shoved his hands into his coat pockets and swallowed. "It's taking all the self-control I have not to haul you into my arms and kiss you. Which would be stupid after what we just went through."

She mirrored him and tucked her hands into her pockets, too. "Maybe I should wait in the tack room until you're finished."

His attention drifted to her mouth and his breathing quickened. "Don't you have lipstick stashed somewhere?"

"In my purse, which I left in the house. Bad move."

"Very bad move. But don't go away." His voice roughened. "I'd rather have you here."

"Okay."

"This won't take long." He stepped back and reached into the tote for a cloth. "I just want to give him a little rubdown. He deserves it."

"That's for sure." As she imagined him doing the same to her, the atmosphere in the barn became too warm for comfort. She tucked her knit cap in her coat pocket and unwound the matching scarf from around her neck.

She shouldn't watch while Jake rubbed the supple cloth over Navarre's coat. It would only remind her of the time he'd gently used a washcloth on her body while they'd stood together in the shower during their memorable night together. Thinking of that, she unbuttoned her coat and took a deep breath.

He moved the cloth over the horse with the same circular motion he'd used when he'd massaged her slick skin. He'd teased her until she'd been wild for him. Then he'd lifted her out of the tub and onto a thick bath mat.

She hadn't quite fit but it hadn't mattered. Slippery as seals, they'd made love on the bathroom floor. They'd laughed like children until they'd been caught in the grip of passion. She'd never come as hard for any man as she did for Jake. Every time.

"What are you thinking about?"

Startled, she opened her eyes. She hadn't realized she'd closed them.

Jake's hands rested on the horse's back as if he'd paused in midmotion when he'd glanced over at her. "Never mind," he said softly. "I have a pretty good idea."

Desire tightened her core. "I—"

"The last time I saw that expression, you were standing in the shower." He wadded up the cloth. "I'm done here." Giving Navarre a final pat, he walked over and dropped the cloth in the caddy. His voice was low as he stood looking at her, his hands shoved firmly in his pockets. "How you tempt me, Amethyst Ferguson."

"I didn't mean to."

"I know. You don't even have to try." He took a shaky

breath. "Would you please put that stuff in the tack room? I'll meet you up there."

"Sure." She grabbed the caddy and walked out of the stall on rubbery legs.

Considering the level of heat they generated, she wondered if they'd be able to lock it down long enough to enjoy the Christmas Eve celebration. He needed to be there but she didn't, so maybe she could feign a headache and go home. Then he could drive to her place once he could get away.

She put the caddy back where she'd found it and took several calming breaths. Much as she'd love to experience Christmas Eve at the ranch house, driving home would be a safer option. She just had to retrieve her purse or ask Jake to bring it to her.

Water started running at the opposite end of the barn, which probably meant Jake was washing his hands prior to going in to the party. No doubt he looked forward to celebrating with his family. She'd been looking forward to it, too, especially because watching him in that setting warmed her heart. She wondered if he'd be disappointed or relieved if she backed out.

The sound of his boots on the wooden barn floor made her heart beat faster. If he affected her that way simply by walking toward her when she couldn't even see his handsome self, how could she expect to behave normally during the party? Instead of satisfying her hunger, the brief episode in the sleigh had whetted her appetite for more.

She stepped out of the tack room. Like her, he'd unbuttoned his coat and he looked determined, like a man on a mission. "Before we leave, we need to discuss something."

"Sure." He stopped a couple of feet away. "Shoot."

That's when she noticed he had a wet bandanna in one hand. Apparently he'd rinsed it out and disposed of the condom. She was glad men had to think of such things and she didn't. "Jake, I have a problem."

"What's that?"

"I can't look at you without fantasizing that we're having sex."

He smiled. "I don't consider that a problem."

"It is when we're hanging out with your family! So I think maybe I should pretend to have a headache and go home. Then you can come to my house when—"

"Whoa, whoa. You want to skip the party?"

"No, I'd love to go, but I'm worried that my thoughts will be written all over my face like they were a while ago."

"You know what? I doubt anyone but me would be able to tell what you were thinking. Don't worry about it."

"They might, and I do worry about it. At least I've figured out why I'm so obsessed. That's some comfort."

His smile widened. "I can't help it if I'm sexy as hell."

"That's not it."

"It's not? Now that's disappointing."

"Well, it sort of is the problem, but the bigger issue is that in August we went straight from having drinks to having an entire night of sex. We didn't interact with anyone."

His eyes darkened and he stepped closer. "Yeah, it was pretty damn hot having all that uninterrupted time to get reacquainted."

"But don't you see? That's what plays in my head when I look at you. I don't know how to be with you in a crowd of people. I just want you alone and naked!" She was alone with him right now but she didn't have any hope that he'd get naked. That didn't mean she wasn't thinking about it.

"Always alone?" His eyebrows lifted. "That could be tricky."

She considered that. "Unrealistic, huh?"

"I guess it could be arranged, but it limits what we can do together." He reached over and fingered a strand of her hair. "I have a different theory."

"What?" Even though he was only touching her hair, she shivered. He also had a telltale gleam in his eyes that she remembered very well.

"We had one amazing night of sex and then didn't see each other for five months. No wonder we're both obsessed with being naked again. We wouldn't be so desperate if we hadn't let so much time go by."

"That makes sense, I guess."

"But that's a future fix, and this is now. I'd like you to be there tonight. We went through a lot of trouble not to muss you up so you could take part in the celebration without being embarrassed."

"True." She swallowed. "But the thing is, I still want you."

"I know." He touched her cheek. "It's written all over your face."

"See?"

"I do, although I still say nobody else would. But we don't have to go inside yet. Let's step into the tack room."

Her breath caught. "Why? You said you didn't have any more—"

"I don't. I left the box in my truck, which is down by the cabin I'm staying in. But that doesn't mean we can't enjoy ourselves." Taking her lightly by the shoulders, he gently backed her through the door. Then he closed and locked it before turning to her. "That's why I washed up." He took off his coat and tossed it aside. Then he helped her out of hers. "I felt a little cheated this afternoon."

Her heart raced and she had trouble getting her breath. "Because you couldn't touch my breasts?"

"Yes, ma'am." He laid her coat across a nearby saddle and hung his hat on the horn. "You have your fantasies and I have mine. Your beautiful breasts are a big part of my memories of that night." He pulled her knit shirt over her head.

Of course she let him do it. Now that he'd begun, she wanted his hands on her, even if that didn't lead to anything. "How will this help?"

"Trust me, it will." After unhooking her bra, he took that off, too. Then he stepped back and sighed. "Even prettier than I remembered." He swallowed. "I never saw you like this." Closing the gap between them, he wrapped one arm around her waist and cradled her breast in his other hand as his hot gaze found hers. "We stripped down so fast and then didn't put on clothes until morning."

She slipped her arms around his neck. "I couldn't get enough of you."

"We couldn't get enough of each other." As he caressed her, he leaned down, his lips nearly making contact. "And this would be the moment when normally I'd kiss you and thrust my tongue deep into your inviting wet mouth. But I can't."

Desire poured like lava through her veins. "There are other places you can kiss me."

"I know." His voice was thick with anticipation. "That

was my plan." Releasing her breast, he hoisted her up and carried her to the shelf where she'd stacked the blankets. "Pull those down."

"I just—"

"I know. Pull them down."

She grabbed the bottom one and jerked so the entire pile tumbled to the floor.

"Perfect." Crouching, he laid her against the mound of blankets. Then he dropped to his knees and braced his hands on either side of her shoulders. "You know what I remember? You giving me directions."

She flushed at the memory of her boldness. "You didn't need them. You know what you're doing."

"I still loved having you tell me what you liked. Tell me again."

"You don't remember?"

"I remember everything. Tell me, anyway." His voice grew husky. "Hearing you say what you want gets me hot."

Reaching up, she combed a lock of silky hair back from his forehead. "I'd never done that before."

"Never?"

"That sexy person everyone thinks I am? It's an act. But that night, with you, it wasn't."

His gaze searched hers. "And now?"

"I like letting go with you, Jake. You make me feel safe."

"And you make me feel a hundred feet tall. I didn't know. I thought…"

"Just you."

Leaning down, he kissed her forehead, her nose and both cheeks before looking into her eyes. "I'm humbled."

She smiled. "But now I'm going to get you hot." Her voice became a soft purr. "Start with your tongue."

His eyes darkened. "Yes, ma'am." He slid lower. "Keep talking."

"Circle slowly to the center," she murmured.

He licked her so sensuously that she squirmed against the blankets and began to pant. "Now take…my nipple into your mouth. Suck gently." She gasped. "Then harder…yes, like that, like *that*. And nip me, Jake. Tug on my…oh, yeah, do that…more…again." The pressure began to build.

His breathing was ragged and his hot breath scorched her skin. "What else? Tell me what you want."

"Make me…make me come."

"Gladly." He unfastened her jeans and pulled the zipper down. In seconds his hand was inside her panties and his fingers began working their magic as he continued to suck hard on her breast.

Oh, yes, she remembered the creative play of Jake's fingers, how he would thrust and twist and press and massage until she lost her mind. She was moments away. "Jake…"

"Don't scare the horses."

"I won't." Gritting her teeth, she arched upward. Not making noise as her body convulsed in a Jake-induced orgasm was a challenge. She managed it with only a few whimpers and soft moans. Then she sank down to the pile of blankets in a grateful heap.

He'd said this would help, and it would certainly help her, but she was worried about how such a passionate episode would affect him. She'd spent many naked hours with this man and surely he was frustrated beyond belief.

After she'd recovered her wits, she asked him. "What about you?"

"Don't think about that. I'll be fine."

"I don't believe you."

"My main concern was you. I don't want you to bail on the Christmas Eve celebration because you're not sexually satisfied. Are you okay now?"

"I feel like a limp rag doll. Is that what you were going for?"

He chuckled. "More or less."

"But that doesn't address your condition. Unless I don't know you at all, you have an erection the size of Devil's Tower."

"Not a problem."

Sliding a hand between them, she fondled him, something she'd loved doing when they'd spent the night together. "I think it is a problem. You're erect and ready to rock and roll. What's your plan for that?"

"I'll control the situation."

"Wrong answer. You just gave me a climax so that I could handle the evening without fixating on you all night. It's only fair that I return the favor."

"But you can't. That would ruin your lipstick."

"Believe me, I so regret not thinking ahead on that score. But help me figure this out, Jake. Tell me what I can do for you."

7

JAKE WANTED AMETHYST with the heat of a thousand suns, especially now when he knew that her uninhibited behavior was a special gift only for him. He'd never dreamed that was the case. Later, when he wasn't so jacked up, he'd take time to think about what it meant.

But at the moment he wasn't thinking at all. She was right about his condition, although he hesitated to take the route that was staring him in the face. He'd waited for a discreet moment to dispose of the condom and rinse out the bandanna. He hadn't had that moment until he'd sent Amethyst to the tack room with the caddy.

The damp bandanna was back in his coat pocket. If Amethyst insisted on somehow evening the score, the bandanna was available. He wasn't sure how he felt about using it. Yet she'd been honest about her needs. Was he going to respond with some macho denial of his? That didn't seem fair, either.

"Just a sec." He got up, retrieved his coat and took out the bandanna. Asking for what he needed wouldn't be easy. He hadn't felt this vulnerable in a very long time. Dropping down beside her on the pile of blankets, he held out the bandanna. "I—" He paused to clear his throat. "I washed this out. You can—"

"Brilliant." Her blue eyes shone. "I certainly can. Lie back."

He stretched out on the blankets with a soft groan. Then he had to clench his jaw against coming as she pulled down his zipper and freed his aching cock.

"I felt a little cheated this afternoon, too," she murmured as she wrapped her warm fingers around the base. "You're magnificent."

"And desperate."

"I know." She began to stroke him with a touch that was light but devastatingly effective.

In no time he began to tremble. Her lipstick issue was minor compared to his idiocy in packing one lone condom. He should have remembered that having her once would only mean he'd want her again, and soon. He should have learned that last summer.

His chest heaved. "Almost…there."

"Don't scare the horses." A hint of laughter rippled through her words.

"Won't." He gasped and swore. *"Now."* Fists clenched, he did his best not to thrust upward, not to yell and not to cuss. He failed in that last part as he came, and came, and came some more. The force of his orgasm was so overwhelming that he barely felt the cool bandanna.

Eyes closed, he lay panting and completely undone. He'd never asked a woman to perform that maneuver. He'd either foregone the pleasure or taken care of it himself once he was alone.

Her breath whispered against his ear. "Be right back." By the time he figured out she was going to rinse out his bandanna, she was already gone. He wondered if she'd traversed the length of the barn topless. Even if she hadn't, he hoped she wouldn't run into anyone.

The horses already had been given their evening meal, which was why he'd decided fooling around in the tack room would go unnoticed. Because it could be locked from the inside and was normally left open, a closed and locked door had come to mean something specific to Thunder Mountain guys.

Zipping his pants and getting to his feet, he noticed that Amethyst's coat was gone but her bra and shirt were still there. She'd obviously hurried to accomplish the chore. That touched him.

She walked in and gave him a smile. "Feeling better?"

He laughed and walked over to her. "Yes, ma'am. The patient is gonna live, after all. Thank you." He caught her around the waist with one hand and reached behind her to lock the door. "Good thing you didn't run into anyone while you were on walkabout."

"I had my story ready. I was going to tell them I had a little motion sickness on the sleigh ride."

"I remember that from high school. No Tilt-A-Whirl for you." He unbuttoned her coat and slipped his hands inside to caress her plump breasts. "Pretty flimsy story, though. A sleigh ride isn't exactly the Tilt-A-Whirl."

"They might have believed me, depending on who it was. I can be very convincing."

"Apparently." He gazed into her eyes and watched them grow smoky with desire as he fondled her. "All along I thought you were way more experienced than me. It seemed so obvious from watching you perform. Your songs can be really hot."

"Sex sells."

"But then we went up to the room and you were amazing in bed. You suggested positions I'd never heard of."

"Because I read." She sighed and leaned into his touch. "With you, I could finally relax and try some of those things I'd read about. And if you keep that up much longer, I'll want to do them with you right here and now."

"So will I." Reluctantly he let her go and stepped back. "We should get going. We've already been gone long enough that someone might start to wonder where we are."

"And come looking for us." She slipped out of her coat and reached for her bra.

She obviously wasn't trying to be provocative by doing that. He'd told her they should get a move on and she was complying. But her unconscious sensuality fired his blood. He turned away, unable to watch her dress without reaching for her. Even the sound of her bra hooks locking into place got to him.

"You're good for my ego, cowboy."

"I hope so." He kept his back to her while he took a steadying breath. "Because you're hell on my package."

"Do you think you'll be able to slip away and drive to my place later tonight?"

His laugh was strained. "That's a priority."

"Did I give you the address last summer?"

"Yep."

"You can turn around. I'm covered up."

He faced her and blew out a breath. "You were right about not having sex in the sleigh. I should have listened to you."

"Why? Do I look mussed, after all?"

"No, you look perfect. That's not the problem. Until we got friendly in the sleigh, I'd convinced myself that having sex with you was great but probably not as great as I remembered. Time plays tricks on us sometimes and we imagine something was better than it actually was."

"But that's not true with us."

"No, it isn't. Which means that instead of throwing myself into this Christmas Eve party, I'll be counting the minutes until I'm in your bed."

She held his gaze. "Me, too, Jake."

AN HOUR LATER Jake felt reasonably in control of himself. He'd managed to hold up his end of conversations without constantly searching the room for Amethyst. As if by mutual agreement they'd spent very little time together but awareness of her was a constant stimulant, as if he'd had way too much caffeine.

Early in the evening Grady Magee had showed up with Amethyst's sister, Sapphire. They were clearly in love and Jake was happy for them, but talking to Sapphire turned out to be a challenge. Certain mannerisms reminded him of Amethyst and as they talked he couldn't shake the notion that she knew about the episode last summer. He couldn't blame Amethyst for confiding in her. In a way it was flattering that she'd wanted to, but that didn't keep him from feeling slightly uncomfortable.

A second beer would have helped, but because of the drive he intended to make after the party wound down, he'd decided not to drink much. He didn't think anyone had noticed until Cade drew him aside.

"Been watching your alcohol intake, Fireman Jake. Or rather, your lack of it." Cade's smile was teasing but there was brotherly concern in his eyes. "Can't help concluding that you have plans tonight."

"I might."

"That sleigh sat empty for quite a while this afternoon."

"Guess so."

"Listen, I get the attraction, bro. Any guy would. But she has big plans."

"I know that. She's very talented."

"Then you're just having a little temporary fun?"

"That's right."

Cade sighed in obvious relief. "Glad to hear it. The way you look at her, I was afraid it was more than that."

"Nope." Jake clapped him on the back. "Not everyone is as focused on that walk down the aisle as you and O'Roarke."

"I know. I wasn't worried that you were that far gone. But you seem to like her and I overheard her telling Chelsea she was seriously thinking she'd give LA a shot."

"Huh." He hadn't seen that coming. The distance between Jackson Hole and Sheridan was an obstacle that could be managed. LA would put her out of reach, but it would definitely give her more opportunities to land the recording contract she wanted.

Putting his selfish motives aside, he should be all for it, but thinking of her going to LA by herself made him uneasy. Did she know anyone there who'd watch out for her and show her the ropes? She was beautiful, and even though her sexy persona was a bluff, it could get her attention from the wrong kind of guy. Sure, that could happen anywhere, but he considered Wyoming a safer bet.

"I take it she hasn't mentioned that to you."

He realized he was scowling and forced himself to relax. "No, but why should she?" He shrugged. "Like you said, we're just having fun. No commitment what-soever."

Cade studied him. "Are you sure? Because I don't think this LA news is sitting well with you."

"Nah, I'm good." He managed a smile.

"Time for presents, you two." Lexi, who'd sprinkled silver glitter in her short, curly hair, walked over and slipped her arm through Cade's. "Everyone's curious about all those hardware store bags, Jake, but since you stapled the top together we can't peek."

"You're not supposed to peek." He gave her a mock glare of disapproval. "You'll ruin the surprise."

"I'll bet I know what it is."

"Bet you don't. So why did you put glitter in your hair? That doesn't seem like a Lexi thing to do."

"Exactly. I wanted to shake things up, be a little more festive this year. Turns out it makes a hell of a mess. I'm shedding glitter everywhere."

"I can testify to that." Cade brushed it off his sleeve.

"Think of it as me showering you with my love."

Cade grinned at her. "Nice save. Now let's go see what Fireman Jake bought us at the hardware store."

Traditionally for the opening of presents, everyone sat on the floor in a wide semicircle around the big tree. Jake felt he could risk choosing a spot next to Amethyst for this part of the evening. The LA plan had cooled his jets somewhat, anyway. He'd thought they'd have a lot more time together in the coming months but maybe not. He'd have to take that into consideration going forward.

Damon brought over a chair for Philomena, although she didn't seem happy about using it. "I appreciate the added comfort," she said, "but I feel kinda funny perched up here above all of you."

Damon gazed up at her from his position on the floor. "I could say you look kinda funny from this angle, too, but—"

"But he won't," Lexi said, "because in his eyes you are the most beautiful, glamorous, mommy-to-be in the world and the queen of his heart. Isn't that right, Damon?"

"Absolutely. That's exactly what I was going to say before you took the words right out of my mouth."

Phil gave him a withering look. "Be careful, daddy-o. My sense of humor disappeared sometime during the third trimester."

"I wouldn't mind having a chair," Rosie said. "I'll sit next to you, Phil. We can be royalty together."

"I'll get it." Herb, who always wore his Santa hat on Christmas Eve, went to fetch Rosie a chair. With his gray hair covered by the cap and a big smile on his face, he looked years younger.

Although Jake hadn't thought he was homesick for the ranch and his foster family, he felt a wave of it as he watched Herb get Rosie settled next to Phil. If the fire department in Sheridan had been hiring when he'd gone looking for a job, he never would have left. Instead he'd ended up in Jackson Hole, which certainly was a beautiful place to live. He liked the people he worked with, too, but Sheridan was home. Maybe he should check on the job situation again and see if he could get back here.

He vividly remembered his first Christmas at the ranch when Herb had explained what he called the November Project. The older guys had jobs in town and could buy small gifts for everyone, but Jake had been fourteen and dead broke. Normally the boys didn't get paid for doing chores, but in November that changed for the younger ones.

Herb found all kinds of odd jobs for them and by the first week in December they each had enough cash to pick out something inexpensive for Rosie, Herb and every foster brother. Herb would take them into town and turn them loose. That first Christmas had been the best one of Jake's life.

As Herb distributed presents and the recipients started opening them, Jake saw that others had chosen his one-size-fits-all solution. Damon and Phil gave everybody eight hours of home maintenance work, collectible after the baby was born. Cade and Lexi had come up with a group trail ride into the mountains next spring complete with a catered lunch.

"You'll have to put in for time off so you can go, too," Cade said to Jake. "And you're welcome to bring a guest." Significantly he didn't suggest bringing Amethyst.

Finn and Chelsea had brought everyone glassware etched with the O'Roarke's logo on one side and a small but sentimental TMB logo on the other. Grady and Sapphire had come up with a creative pairing of their skills. Sapphire had made colorful serving platters, no two alike, and Grady had designed a decorative metal holder so they could hang on the wall when not in use.

Jake's smoke alarms brought laughter but sincere thanks, too.

"This is a very loving gift," Rosie said. "Thank you, Jake."

"I really need this." Amethyst smiled at Jake. "Thank you. I've been meaning to ask the landlady to replace ours with a better one, but now I don't have to."

"You're welcome." He gave her a quick smile. Damn

it, now when he looked at her he couldn't help thinking she could be gone in a matter of weeks. Earlier he'd worried that he should have bought her something more personal, but now he was glad he hadn't. He'd be wise to dial back on the sentimentality.

"I apologize that I have no gifts for any of you," Amethyst said. "But if you're up for a song, I could give you that."

"That would be lovely," Rosie said.

"Definitely." Lexi got to her feet. "But before Amethyst gives us a song, I have a special gift for Cade."

Jake held his breath. This had damn well better be a proposal.

"Should I stand up?" Cade's heart was in his eyes.

Jake *really* wanted this to be a proposal.

"Yes." Lexi took a deep breath. "Please."

Cade got to his feet. To Jake's surprise, the guy was steady as a rock while Lexi seemed a little shaky.

She reached in her pocket and pulled out a small jewelry box. Then she dropped to one knee. "Cade Gallagher, I love you more than life itself and I would be honored if you would agree to marry me." She popped open the box, which contained a man's gold wedding band.

He peered at it. "I can't put that on yet, can I?"

"Not yet. It's for the ceremony." Lexi's jaw tightened. "But I couldn't very well give you a diamond engagement ring. So what's your answer?"

Cade rubbed his chin. "I'm thinking."

"Cade Gallagher, if you don't accept this proposal I swear I'll…"

"What?"

"Get glitter all over you!"

"Ah, Lexi, you will anyway." Reaching down, he pulled her to her feet. "You know I'll marry you, woman. Thank God you finally asked." And he kissed her as everyone in the room stood and cheered.

Sometime in the middle of all that Jake had taken Amethyst's hand. What a stupid thing to do.

But she laced her fingers through his and gave his hand a squeeze. "I love this," she murmured.

"Yeah, me, too." And the worst part was, the scene with Cade and Lexi had showed him that he wanted more from Amethyst than she was willing to give.

8

JAKE'S BEHAVIOR TOWARD her had changed and Amethyst wasn't sure why. He'd pulled back, retreated into some kind of protective shell that reminded her of their high school days. Then he'd taken her hand during Lexi's memorable proposal and she'd thought maybe things were okay, after all.

They weren't, though. The minute the kiss had ended and Cade had called for champagne, Jake had released her hand.

"I need to go help," he'd murmured before hurrying toward the kitchen.

She'd thought it was an excuse, but now wasn't the time to ask him what was going on.

Champagne flowed and everyone congratulated the newly engaged couple. Amethyst felt out of sorts but she knew how to fake looking like a party girl. When Rosie reminded her that she'd promised everyone a song, she asked Cade and Lexi what they'd like to hear. After all, this was their special night.

They picked a sentimental tune from their senior prom and she sang it a cappella, giving it all she had.

Halfway through she glanced at Jake. He looked destroyed. Obviously the happy fling they'd planned was no longer going smoothly. She wondered if he'd changed his mind about driving to her house tonight.

If he had, she might never find out what the deal was. Talk about déjà vu. He'd acted this way in high school and she'd had to pry the reason out of him, which had turned out to be that she'd supposedly flirted with another guy.

That couldn't be the situation tonight. Every man in the room was taken and she wouldn't have cared if a gorgeous eligible male had appeared. She was with Jake. Until recently she'd thought he was with her, too. Now she wasn't so sure.

Eventually she maneuvered him into a quiet corner and asked him the pertinent question. "Are you still planning to drive to my house?"

His reply was short and to the point. "Yes."

"Is something wrong?"

"I don't know. Is there?"

She got right in his face. "Don't do that, Jake Ramsey. Don't answer a question with another question. Is something bothering you? If so, spit it out."

"Cade told me you were going to LA."

Aha. That explained it. "I'm *thinking* about it. Nothing's been decided." She liked Cade, but she wished he'd kept his mouth shut.

"But that's what you ultimately need to do, isn't it?"

"Quite possibly. Chelsea's comments made me realize I should consider it. She's a marketing whiz and I need to listen to her. Then Rosie told me about Matt Forrest, who took off for LA three years ago and, after toughing it out, he's up for a major role. I began asking myself if

I'm being cowardly to keep performing in my Wyoming safety zone in hopes someone will discover me here."

"Do you have contacts in LA?"

"Not yet. That's the purpose of going, to make some. Hire an agent."

"But what if you run into some sleazy characters? What if they make promises they never plan to deliver? What if they—?"

"I'm not seventeen years old, Jake. I've learned something about judging people and making good business decisions. I might have fallen for some fast-talker when I was younger, but I'm not as gullible now."

His chest heaved. "I'm sure you're not."

"I promise I'll be smart about things." She searched his gaze and saw the uncertainty there. He was concerned about her on a more visceral level and she got that. She was a small-town girl considering a move to the big city. "Look, I'm not leaving next week. Probably not even next month."

"But you will go."

"After listening to Chelsea, I think I should if I'm serious about my career." She took a steadying breath. "I realize that affects…us."

"There is no *us*."

"Yes, there is, Jake. We might not have planned it that way last summer, but clearly what we feel for each other goes beyond sex. We might as well acknowledge that and deal with it."

"What's to deal with? You're leaving. End of story."

Although he sounded angry, he was probably mostly worried about her and maybe a little hurt, too. He wouldn't want to admit that last part, especially in the middle of a family party. "Tell you what. I'll go tell everyone goodbye and head on out. You probably want some private time with your brothers."

He sighed and rubbed the back of his neck. "Hey, I'm sorry. Don't go yet. We'll drop the subject."

"I'm not leaving in a huff," she said softly. "I don't do that."

He gave her a rueful smile. "No, I do that."

"Sometimes." She touched his cheek. "I really think it's time for me to go home."

He looked as if he might want to argue, but then he nodded. "I'll get your coat while you make the rounds."

"Thanks." Amethyst made her way through the room collecting hugs and Christmas wishes. Grady and Sapphire said they'd see her tomorrow and Sapphire gave her an extra hug and a whispered "good luck."

Jake waited by the front door loaded down with her stuff, including the bag containing the smoke alarm. That gift made her smile. Naturally he had his coat and hat on, too. She would have been surprised if he hadn't walked her to her car. He was both gallant and protective.

He was also beautiful to look at. As she came toward him, her heart stalled. He'd been a cutie-pie in high school, but since then his shoulders had broadened and his chest had filled out. His face had lost its smooth-cheeked boyishness in favor of rugged masculinity emphasized by the slight shadow of his beard. He fought fires for a living, a heroic job she'd always admired, and tonight his sheepskin coat and gray Stetson added a layer of cowboy appeal.

Moving a thousand miles away from Jake wasn't going to be easy. The miles would be a major barrier between them, but the psychological distance would be the relationship killer. Living in LA would change her in ways she probably couldn't imagine. She'd told him the move wasn't imminent, but the longer she delayed, the tougher she'd make it on both of them. As a kid she'd preferred ripping off a bandage to end the pain faster.

He helped her on with her coat before handing over her purse. "I don't know what was going through your mind just now, but you didn't look happy."

"Just thinking that transitions aren't a lot of fun." She hooked her purse strap across her body.

"Nope."

"But it's the only way to grow." She wound the scarf around her neck and reached for the hat he held out.

"Assuming you choose the right ones."

"Which is something you can't always know in advance." She pulled on her hat and took her gloves from her coat pocket.

"Guess not. I'll carry your smoke alarm." He pulled on his gloves before opening the door. Cold air slammed into them as they both hurried out and he wrapped his free hand around her shoulders. "Be careful on the steps. They're slippery."

She considered telling him that she had slippery porch steps, too, and she'd been navigating them just fine on her own, but she didn't have the heart. Jake's protective instincts ran deep and were the main reason he'd chosen to become a firefighter. No wonder the thought of her going off to LA alone was pushing all his buttons.

But maybe they'd be able to talk it through. "Look, I know you're not crazy about my plan."

"I'm not, and it might seem like I'm being selfish, but there's more to it than that." Their boots crunched through the frozen snow as they walked to her SUV.

"This may sound chauvinistic, but I'm not convinced LA is a safe place for a single woman who doesn't know anybody, let alone one who looks like you."

She didn't know if it was chauvinistic but it sounded exactly like Jake. If he could manage it he'd send her with a bodyguard. "Have you ever been to LA?"

"Actually, I have. Several of us went for training in crowd control. Jackson Hole is getting more popular with celebrities all the time, and our chief wants us to be prepared in case a situation gets out of hand."

She had to admit that gave his opinion more weight. Other than a family trip when she was a kid, she'd never been. "Did you consider it a dangerous city?"

"Not if you're hanging out with a bunch of firefighters."

They'd reached her SUV and she turned to face him while she dug in her purse for her keys. "Would you feel better if I took a self-defense course?"

"Yes. But mostly I wish you knew someone there."

She found her keys and glanced up at him. "I just thought of something. I do know somebody. Matt. Rosie could put us in touch. I'll bet he'd have all kinds of tips on living in LA."

"You should definitely contact him, but you'd better do it soon. Rosie said if he gets the part he'll be shooting on location in Utah for the next few months."

"I hadn't heard that. So much for that brainstorm."

"Maybe he won't get the part, but if he does, you could hold off going until he's back."

She hated seeing the spark of hope in his green eyes because she was about to douse it. "I don't think that's a good idea."

His jaw tightened. "Then you'd better sign up for a self-defense class."

"I'll look into it." Taking hold of his arms for balance, she stood on tiptoe and dipped under his hat to give him a quick kiss. Belatedly she realized a peck on the lips probably wouldn't satisfy either of them, even if they were standing in sub-zero weather.

Sure enough, he groaned and pulled her close. Then he angled his head so he could kiss her more thoroughly without losing his hat.

She'd forgotten that he'd perfected that technique when they'd dated in high school. His kisses had been hot then, too, but he'd never completely lost control, much to her disappointment. Tonight all restraint was gone. Backing her against the side of her SUV, he thrust his tongue deep.

She gripped the collar of his coat and hung on as he ravished her mouth. He poured equal parts longing and frustration into a kiss that surrounded them in a cloud of steam. His arms shielded her from the cold metal of the SUV, but he was still holding the smoke alarm and it pressed against the small of her back. She was sandwiched between the alarm on one side and his erection on the other. Great sex and constant vigilance—the two elements epitomized Jake Ramsey.

The cold air lost its punch as she began to heat up. She imagined opening the door and making love in the backseat. If he'd thought to bring a condom out here, she could easily be talked into it.

Panting, he lifted his mouth from hers. "God, how I want you."

"Let me open the car. We can—"

"Not *here*." His laughter was choked. "Damn, woman,

they'd find our frozen bodies in the morning if we tried a stunt like that. But I'm so done with this party." He released her and stepped back, his chest heaving. "Stay here with the motor running while I let everyone know I'm following you home."

"You are? I thought you'd want to stay longer and hang out with your family."

"I thought so, too, but I have a more urgent issue that needs to be dealt with. I'll be with them in the morning while you're at your folks' house. Get in the car and wait for me. I'll be out in a sec." He handed her the bag and backed away.

She gulped. "Okay, if you say so."

"I do. When you see my truck's headlights, pull out ahead of me." He turned and started for the ranch house, his long strides covering the frozen ground much faster than when he'd been walking with her.

She gazed after him until the cold penetrated her sensual fog and she began to shiver. Without his warmth encircling her, the breeze sliced right through her coat. Climbing into her SUV, she tossed her purse and gift bag on the passenger seat. Then she started the motor and continued to shiver while she waited for it to warm up so she could turn on the heater.

His headlights swung into view not long after she'd done that. He'd really hustled to get here so fast. Putting the SUV in gear, she pulled out ahead of him and started down the winding road that led to the highway.

Once they reached the main road, driving to her place became a kind of vehicular foreplay. Hardly anyone was out at this hour on Christmas Eve, so she could concentrate on the headlights in her rearview mirror and picture Jake impatiently waiting for the moment they were alone in her house.

He'd said the box of condoms was in his truck. He'd likely bring some in with him but if not she'd bought his favorite brand this morning. Thanks to their interlude in Jackson Hole she knew what that was. They'd had to make a trip to the gift shop before heading up to her room.

Judging from his comments today, he'd been under the impression she was used to spontaneous sexual encounters while on the road. Although she'd had plenty of offers, she'd never taken a man to her hotel room after a performance until she'd invited Jake. She'd only done it then because she'd known him.

She'd expected to have fun because they'd always had chemistry. She hadn't expected to have such an incredible sexual experience that she'd turned down every guy who'd asked her out since then. Without consciously admitting it, she'd been saving herself for Jake. That made no sense, especially now that she'd pretty much decided to move to LA.

Or maybe it did make sense. She'd laid all her cards on the table so he knew she was career focused and he wanted her anyway, for whatever time they could be together. He'd initially questioned her new plan but now he seemed to have accepted it provided she got some martial arts training.

That left them free to enjoy passionate sex for the next couple of nights. She'd forgotten to ask him when he had to drive back, but if he'd been given the holiday off he wouldn't be leaving until at least the twenty-sixth. That was more time with Jake than she'd had last summer and she was grateful.

The two-story Victorian that she now shared with Arlene was dark inside. When she'd left earlier today she'd planned to come back, change clothes and freshen up before the party at Thunder Mountain. But the multicolored Christmas lights she'd draped along the porch railing were on a timer so they were glowing and illuminated the fresh pine wreath she'd hung on the front door.

She'd also figured on having an opportunity after the party to prepare a seductive welcome for Jake by turning on the Christmas tree lights and lighting some scented candles. That hadn't happened, either, but judging from the way he'd kissed her, he wouldn't need atmosphere to get him in the mood.

She pulled into the driveway and left enough space for him to park behind her. Anticipation tightened her chest and sent her pulse into the red zone. Until now they'd had to be somewhat cautious, but once they were inside her house, they had almost no restrictions.

They'd have more freedom tonight than they'd had in her hotel room. Her windows were closed and so were her neighbors'. They could yell all they wanted.

By the time she opened her door and climbed out holding her purse and her gift bag, he was there to grab her hand and tug her toward the porch. "Got the key?"

She held it up.

"Perfect. Your lights are festive, by the way."

She laughed. "I'm surprised you noticed."

"I'm trying not to behave like a sex-starved man."

"I appreciate the effort."

"What kind of flooring do you have?"

"Hardwood. Is that a firefighter kind of question?"

"No."

"Then it's a weird thing to ask me, Jake."

"Not if you're in my condition. I need to know if the floor would work or if the sofa is a better option. Do you have a sofa?"

"Yes, and you're insane." She opened the door.

"I'll admit to it." He propelled her through the door and kicked it shut. "Oh, good, you have a rug. Come here."

"Jake, this is crazy. My bedroom's just up the—" But the trip upstairs that she'd been about to suggest became a moot point as his eager mouth captured hers. She dropped her purse and the smoke alarm as he pulled her down to the flowered carpet she'd found on sale last year.

After getting it home, she'd been pleased with how it echoed the Victorian theme of the house. She'd never envisioned that she'd be pinned to it while a virile cowboy unzipped her jeans and thrust his hand inside her panties, but she enjoyed that maneuver.

She enjoyed it even more when his nimble fingers coaxed an orgasm from her quivering body. As she lay gasping from that unexpected pleasure, he pulled off her boots and divested her of her underwear and jeans. Then he lifted her hips and gave her another climax, this time using his mouth and tongue with devastating effect. But she was still wearing her shirt, her bra, her coat, her scarf, her gloves and her knit hat.

She tore off the gloves and hat and tossed them away, but that didn't solve the issue. "I'm burning up." She unbuttoned her coat and yanked her scarf from around her neck.

"Me, too." A zipper rasped in the darkness followed by the crinkle of foil.

"No, really, I'm burning up. The top of me is dressed for a blizzard and the bottom of me is in Tahiti."

"Oh." Breathing hard, he loomed over her. "I see."

She reached up and gripped his sheepskin coat. "Don't you want to take all this off before we continue?"

"Okay." Sitting back on his heels, he wrenched off his coat and tossed it aside. Something spilled out of the pockets that sounded like a barrage of condoms. Then he helped her sit up so she could wiggle out of her coat.

"I have a nice bed upstairs."

"Couldn't make it. Grab on to me."

His desperation sent lust spiraling through her again. She got a grip on his shoulders and he spanned her waist with his big hands. His upper body strength allowed him to lift and position her so his cock nudged the spot where his mouth had recently given her such pleasure. Then he let gravity take over.

She'd never loved a sensation more than she loved this one. There were other techniques for getting and giving satisfaction and they'd tried quite a few. But as Jake slowly filled the aching space that was so ready for him, she felt a special joy that only happened when they connected in this basic way. Once her knees reached the floor, she was able to help him create that sweet friction they both craved.

He groaned. "So good."

"Mmm." She moved faster, yearning for the climax that hovered just out of reach.

His breathing roughened and he tightened his hold on her hips. "Slow down."

"Don't want to."

"I'll come."

"That's the idea." She dug her fingers into his shoulders. "Turn me loose."

With a soft oath he let go and she rode him fast, and faster yet, until she came in a rush. The moment she did, he thrust upward with a strangled cry of triumph. He held her in place as his cock pulsed and he gasped for air.

Gradually their bodies relaxed and they sagged against each other until their breathing quieted. Then Jake began to chuckle.

Leaning back, she looked at him. "What's so funny?"

"Me. I barely made it through the damn door before I was on you. I'm pretty sure I scattered condoms everywhere. Not particularly cool of me."

"I like it when you lose your cool." She cupped his face and gave him a tender kiss. "Remember August? Remember what happened the minute we got into the room?"

"I backed you up against the nearest wall and we did it standing up. Couldn't make it to the bed that was only ten feet away. You make me go wild."

"How does that feel?"

"Great." He took her mouth gently, almost reverently, before lifting his head again. "Thank you for inspiring me to go nuts."

"My pleasure." Maybe this was what Jake needed from her, the chance to abandon his cautious nature and surrender to his underlying sensuality. She'd known all along it was there. She'd had a small taste of it when they'd been teenagers and she'd had solid confirmation now that they'd shared hours of adult pleasure.

How ironic that she wasn't any bolder than Jake and yet, because he'd believed she was, he'd become more sexually adventurous. That might carry over into his next relationship or it might not. Until now she'd avoided imagining him with someone else but she had to be realistic. If she didn't want to be tied down, then of course he'd move on. What a depressing thought that was!

9

JAKE STILL COULDN'T believe his lack of restraint with Amethyst. Mr. Smooth he was not and now he had a little problem. "Wild and crazy is fun and all, but it's left me sitting in the middle of your fairly dark living room wondering where I can dispose of the—"

"Oh!" She gently lifted her hot body away from his. "Stay put. I'll bring you a trash can and a box of tissues." She was back in no time. "There you go."

"Thanks." His eyes had adjusted so he could see a little better, but fortunately he could do this job blindfolded. Getting to his feet, he took care of the condom. Then he pulled up his briefs and zipped his jeans.

"Don't you want to just take everything off? I'm still roasting."

He glanced over at her and noticed she'd taken off her shirt. "And walk around your house naked?"

"Sure. Ah, that feels so much better." She whipped off her bra, too. "I really worked up a sweat."

"If you're going to strip I want to be able to see you. Mind if I turn on a lamp?"

"No, but I have a better idea." She walked over to the

shadowy branches of the Christmas tree she'd placed in front of the windows that looked out on the porch.

Seconds later colored lights bloomed on the Christmas tree and bathed her in a rainbow that took his breath away. "You're gorgeous."

She smiled. "I love being naked with you, Jake. Take off the rest of your clothes, okay?"

He thought about it. "Not gonna work for me."

"Why not? You were fine being naked in the hotel room."

"That's different. We were either in bed or in the shower most of the time. Here we have an entire house to have sex in."

"So what?"

"We can do it anywhere." And the longer he looked at her, the more ideas he had. "On the kitchen table, on the stairs, in the hallway, against the front door, under the Christmas tree, up against the—"

"Okay, I get the idea, but if you're naked that makes those episodes so much easier."

"The shirt can go, and the boots, but not the jeans. I need pockets." Speaking of which, he needed to reload. Sure enough, the carpet was littered with condoms. He gathered them up and transferred several to his jeans before putting the rest in his coat pocket.

She watched him with a smile on her face. "Think you have enough, there?"

"Maybe not." But he sat on the sofa so he could pull off his boots and socks. They definitely weren't necessary.

"I have more of those little raincoats upstairs in my bedroom, where the bed is, hint, hint."

"Patience." He dropped a boot on the floor and glanced up with a lazy grin. "We'll get there."

That made her laugh. "See, you're not the only eager one around here. And I admit I hadn't thought of the storage issue, especially if you want to have sex all over the house."

"It's not your job to cover the equipment." And his equipment was really interested in some action now that she was standing there in the glow of those Christmas lights. Her silky skin was dappled in soft shades of red, green, yellow and blue. He committed the image to memory because chances were good he wouldn't be enjoying this view a year from now.

As he stood and walked toward her, he noticed that her nipples were rigid. Could be either a response to him or to the temperature. "Are you cold?"

"A little, now that we're not having sex. I guess we can't exactly be doing it *all* the time."

"Now there's a challenge." He pulled her into his arms. "Can I keep you heated up enough that you don't feel the need to put on clothes? I just might take that challenge."

"No, don't. It sounds exhausting." She gave him a quick kiss. "Let me throw on something that's a good compromise. I know what I need. It's in a basket of clean laundry on top of the dryer. Want to come with me to fetch it?"

"You bet. Then I can check your wiring."

She batted her eyelashes at him. "Mmm, laundry room sex. What sort of position do you need me in so you can check my wiring?"

He groaned. "Any position works to get me hot. But you'll hate hearing I meant the wiring in your house."

"Well, damn."

"But after that I'll be happy to check out your personal wiring."

"Okay, then." She tossed a smile over her bare shoulder as she sashayed through her kitchen and into the small room adjacent to it.

He took a quick glance at the kitchen on the way through. It looked recently remodeled, which was a good sign if the remodelers had known what they were doing. He'd check it out later, but apparently they'd installed refurbished antique appliances. Nice touch.

Amethyst flipped on an overhead light and gestured toward her washer and dryer. "Check away."

He leaned over the back to study the outlets. "They're fine. Sometimes older houses aren't set up to handle newer machines but this one seems to be. I'm assuming you clean out the lint trap regularly."

"Yes, Fireman Jake, I clean out the lint trap regularly."

"Good." He turned around to find her wearing a red flannel sleep shirt trimmed in faux white fur. Although it covered her up, knowing she wore nothing under it created a whole new level of tension.

She walked over and snuggled against him. "You like?" She lifted her face to his.

"Sure do. It's very soft." Reaching down, he pulled up the fur-trimmed hem so he could fondle her firm little butt. "But you're softer."

"And you're harder." She wiggled against him. "I can feel your pride and joy. Did you want to check my wiring?"

"I do." He leaned down and nuzzled the curve of her neck. "I really do, but I also want to evaluate the appliances in your kitchen. I promise to make it fast."

"So I'm getting my own personal safety check?" She massaged his chest in slow, sensuous strokes.

"That's the idea." He breathed in the coconut scent of her shampoo. Coconut had become a trigger that made him think of her long, dark hair sweeping over his naked body. "If I can keep my mind on the subject."

"You'll feel better once you've made sure I'm not living with any fire hazards, won't you?"

"Yes." He forced himself to stop nibbling on her smooth shoulder and lift his head.

She stepped back. "Then let's take care of that. I want you to feel loose and carefree, not uptight about any dangers lurking in my house."

"You don't know how much I appreciate that."

"I think I do. You're very sweet, Jake."

"Sweet?" He winced. "You sure know how to hurt a guy."

"It's a compliment!"

"Not to a member of the Thunder Mountain Brotherhood. We prefer strong and courageous." He grinned. "But I'm sure you meant well. Let's go look at your retro kitchen."

She turned and led the way. "I love it. The landlady wanted it to appear as if it might be more than a hundred years old, and in some ways it does. I feel as if I step back in time when I come in here."

"I wonder if women a hundred years ago used to walk through their kitchens naked."

She leaned against the counter, temptation personified. "Depends on whether they were lucky enough to have a lusty man who enjoyed watching them do it."

"That counter is the perfect height for..."

"What?"

He blew out a breath. "Never mind." With great effort he looked away from her seductive smile and continued his inspection of the kitchen. "It's well-done. No complaints."

"Want to see my roommate's area?"

No. But once he'd realized she lived in an older house his first thought had been faulty wiring. If he didn't check it out, he wouldn't be doing his job as a firefighter. "Might as well cover the entire bottom floor before we head upstairs." That was another issue he had with her moving to LA. She wouldn't have a lot of money and rents were high. She could end up living in some firetrap because it was all she could afford. "If you ever think of renting a place and the windows are painted shut, please don't move in, okay?"

"I won't."

He made a cursory examination of the bedroom her roommate Arlene used and he found no frayed cords or overloaded outlets. "Looking good. Upstairs we go."

She preceded him up the wooden staircase. "I'm glad I've passed inspection so far."

He couldn't respond to that because he was mesmerized by the view as he followed her. The soft flannel outlined her body and aroused him almost beyond his endurance. The possibilities of the staircase taunted him. They could connect on multiple levels and create all kinds of positions. He filed the information away for later because he really wanted to check out the second floor. That's where Amethyst spent most of her time and a person could become trapped in such a situation.

Her bedroom was the primary source of concern because she slept alone up here—at least, that's how he preferred to picture it—and she might not be aware of a fire breaking out on the first floor. He studiously avoided looking at her bed while he opened the window to make sure it was functional.

Closing it quickly to shut out the cold air, he pulled the curtains closed and turned to her. "If you had a fire and the stairs were blocked, you could climb out this window and onto the front porch roof."

She gazed at the window as if imagining the scenario. "You know, I never thought of that."

"Then I'm glad I mentioned it. Sometimes in an emergency we don't think of the obvious. If you had to, I'll bet you could hang from the porch roof and drop to the ground without doing major damage to yourself."

"I'm sure I could." Her blue eyes darkened. "You're really sexy when you're being official."

He tossed that off with a laugh because he hadn't finished his inspection. If he responded to the invitation in her gaze, he never would. They'd wear each other out in the bed that was steps away and then fall into an exhausted sleep. "I'm not trying to be sexy. I'm trying to—"

"Keep me safe. I know. I guess what I'm saying is that this job you have, where you protect people from the dangers of fire, is super important. Watching you look at everything with a practiced eye turns me on."

"Nice to know." His cock began to throb. "If I remember right, you made the other bedroom into a studio."

"I did. It's at the back of the house." She led the way down the hall and pointed out the bathroom on the way. "I promise I have no frayed cords dangling anywhere."

"I believe you."

"But this is the smoke alarm I'd like to replace with

the one you gave me." She gestured toward the ceiling of the hall.

He glanced up at it. "Yeah, that's definitely an older model. I'll replace it before I leave in the morning."

"Thank you. I don't have your diligence but I wasn't kidding about wanting a better one. I spend most of my time up here." She walked through the doorway at the end of the hall and flipped on a light. "This is where the magic happens, or what I hope is magic. Time will tell."

When he walked in, he was hit by the dedication to her craft that had produced this studio. He didn't know a lot about electronics but he suspected her setup had required some serious money. Besides the recording equipment and two computers, she had an elaborate keyboard that looked expensive. Several autographed pictures of popular singers decorated the walls. He circled the room to read the names and recognized some but not all.

"I was the opening act for a few of the lesser known ones," she said. "The really famous ones are from my fan-girl days when I went to every concert within driving distance."

"This is impressive, Amethyst. I can tell a lot of effort went into creating it."

"It did. Finding the equipment at a reasonable price wasn't easy, but then I had to get the landlady's permission to soundproof the room. And before you ask, the panel over the window lifts off. I realize now that I could climb out that one, too. There's even a little porch roof over the back stoop, although the thought of a fire never occurred to me. I just wanted to be able to open the window on nice days when I'm composing but not recording."

"I feel a lot better about you spending so much time

on the second floor." He shoved his hands into his pockets so he wouldn't reach for her. Being here in her studio surrounded by the evidence of her talent forced him to see the heartbreaking truth. She needed to make her bid for the big-time. Sure, he'd be worried about her when she went to LA, but only a very selfish person would try to talk her out of going.

"I love it up here, especially now that I have my studio organized. I can work any time of the day or night and not disturb anyone. But the outlay was substantial, so that's when I decided to give voice lessons to bring in more cash." Her expression became more animated. "The kids are a riot and they *love* this studio. We put together a Christmas album they're each giving to their folks."

"Great idea. Could you give voice lessons in LA to bring in more money?"

"Maybe. I wouldn't have the same setup, though, and here it's easy to get students because a lot of people already know me. There isn't much competition." She smiled. "This fall one kid's mom took a few lessons because she wanted to sing 'Santa Baby' to her husband on Christmas Eve. I guess people remember that Christmas show."

"I sure do. I watched you perform that song and cussed myself out for being a damned fool."

"You could have said something."

"Yeah, I know." He sighed. "But I'd never expected to hold on to you for long, anyway. I figured you were too hot for me."

"Oh, Jake." She walked over to him and slid her hands up his bare chest. "But I can't blame you for not recognizing it was all for show. I didn't want anybody to see through me, not even you. I still put on that sexy girl persona like a suit of armor before every performance. It let's me go out there without being scared."

He put his arms around her and massaged the small of her back. "Thank you for letting me in on the secret."

She gazed up at him with a sparkle in her blue eyes. "I have an idea."

"Me, too." He smiled. "I wonder if it's the same idea."

"Probably not. I want to sing you a song."

"You do?" He hadn't seen that coming.

"Sit right here in my office chair." She led him to a cushy black-leather chair on rollers.

He settled into it. "What song?"

"You'll see." Stepping away from him, she cleared her throat and moistened her lips. "I've never performed this without accompaniment, but it could be better that way. More intimate." Looking into his eyes, she began singing in a soft, sultry voice.

He should have known the minute she'd suggested it what she'd choose for her serenade. Gripping the arms of the chair, he vowed that he would not leave it until she was finished, no matter how hot he became. And guaranteed he would become very hot for her. No one could sing "Santa Baby" like Amethyst.

10

AMETHYST HAD NEVER tried to seduce a man with a private solo, but, wow, was it effective. Jake had a death grip on the arms of that chair and his powerful chest rose and fell more rapidly with each stanza. This was way more fun than she'd imagined it would be.

Quite a bit was going on behind his fly, too. She couldn't resist teasing him even more by perching on his knee and running her fingers through his hair as she sang. Then she toyed with his chest hair and lightly pinched his nipples.

His low moan of pleasure nearly caused her to abandon the performance. She didn't want to do that, but she was turning herself on, too, and her normal breathing techniques weren't working very well. Fortunately the song was supposed to be delivered in a breathy, slightly husky voice. She certainly had that down.

Toward the end, when she was afraid she'd end up gasping out the last lines because she needed him so desperately, her professional pride kicked in. She regained control of her breathing long enough to finish with the cute, pouty ending, a final touch that made his eyes darken and his nostrils flare.

Desire pulsed within her and tightened a coil of need that demanded release. If he didn't take her in the next five minutes, she might burst into flames all on her own. Quivering, she brushed a kiss over his mouth. "Thanks for listening."

In response he scooped her into his arms and stood, kicking the chair away as he strode out of the room and down the hall.

"Did you like it?"

His reply was strained and succinct. "Yes."

Judging from the way he was barreling down the hall toward her bedroom, she almost expected him to throw her down on the bed. Instead he laid her on the comforter with exquisite tenderness and gently worked her out of her fur-trimmed sleep shirt. No movement was wasted, though, as he pulled a condom from his pocket and shucked his jeans and briefs. He was obviously a man on a mission.

He rolled on the condom before climbing into bed and moving between her thighs.

Looking into his eyes, she found the heat she knew would be there, but another emotion lurked in his steady gaze, one far more potent. Her heart answered with a surge of fierce joy, even though allowing such feelings to take root was a huge mistake for both of them. She stroked his muscled back and felt him tremble beneath her touch. "I'm glad you liked my song."

He started to speak but had to pause to clear his throat. "I didn't just like it. I loved it. And, dear God, how I need you." He plunged his cock deep.

She arched off the bed, a wild cry of joy rising from

her throat as Jake pounded into her again and again. The bed rocked with the force of his thrusts. She lost control in seconds and clung to him as her world shattered into a million brilliant pieces. With a roar that echoed off the walls of her small bedroom, he drove in once more and his big body shuddered in the aftermath of his climax. Gasping for breath, he remained braced above her with his eyes squeezed shut.

At last he opened them, but he still looked dazed. He shook his head as if to clear it. "I have never...wanted anyone so much."

When she reached up to cup his cheek she felt the prickly beginnings of his beard. "I guess it was the song."

"Not just the song, although it really got to me." He took a shaky breath. "It's knowing you've let down your guard for the first time and I'm the lucky SOB you've chosen to do that with. Knowing what you've told me about your suit of armor, I'd bet my badge you've never performed that song for a guy before."

"Nope. Just you."

"That's a powerful aphrodisiac."

She smiled. "Apparently."

"Take my word for it." He leaned down and gave her a gentle kiss. "Don't go away. I'd like to wash up a little."

"I remember that about you. And I can't imagine why I'd leave when I have a seriously ripped fireman spending Christmas Eve in my bed."

His gaze flickered. "Glad I could be here." Easing away from her, he left the bed and walked out into the hall.

While he was gone she got up and pulled the covers back. After all, she'd bought sheets decorated with brightly wrapped Christmas packages so she might as well make the rest of the evening festive. She hadn't expected anyone to enjoy the holiday bedding except her, but after meeting Jake in the hardware store she'd washed everything and put it back on.

She considered lighting the candles she'd arranged on her dresser but after being around Jake in this setting she realized he might not be enamored of that plan. She'd ask him when he came back. In the meantime she could turn her bedside lamp down a notch before stretching out on her Christmas-themed linens.

When he walked into the bedroom looking his usual manly self, she was reminded again of their rendezvous in Jackson Hole. She'd loved having a chance to admire and explore his body that night. Now she had another golden opportunity.

He glanced at the bedding and grinned. "Don't tell me you bought the sheets after we talked in the hardware store."

"Nope. Picked them up a few weeks ago, but they're freshly laundered for the occasion." She gestured toward the dresser. "I have candles, but now I'm thinking you might not be a fan."

He looked over at the dresser. "I'm not crazy about candles in the bedroom. Dinner by candlelight is one thing, but we could forget these were burning. I don't know about you, but I forget my own name when we're—"

"Say no more. We need to concentrate on orgasms, not candles."

"Thank you for that." He climbed into bed beside her. "These sheets remind me I didn't wrap your present up nice and fancy."

"I don't care. The smoke alarm is perfect. Besides, the best gift is you, and I like you much better unwrapped." She ran her fingers through his thick hair. "I remember your hair as being lighter."

"I'd been out in the sun a lot. Did some hiking in the Tetons." As if following her lead, he picked up a lock of her hair and drew it over her shoulder. "Did you cut some off? It used to reach to your nipple. I remember tickling you with it."

"It's a little shorter. Now I wish I hadn't cut it."

"That's okay. It'll grow back." Then he paused, as if realizing he wouldn't necessarily be around once it did. "I mean—"

"For New Year's I'll bring feathers."

He shook his head and grinned. "You'd do it, too."

"I would. I've never played around with feathers but it could be fun. Maybe I'll bring a little satchel of stuff, get creative."

"Mmm, I like that idea." He lazily brushed his finger over her nipple. "I hope I can get the night off. I can't remember for sure, but I'll bet the chief scheduled me for New Year's Eve. It wasn't important so I didn't notice before I left."

"It doesn't matter if you'll let me stay in your apartment when I drive over. I can hang around until you're off duty."

"You'd do that?"

"Why not? Driving to Jackson Hole and not seeing you makes no sense, especially if I don't have to pay for extra nights at the hotel."

"Of course you can stay with me. I'd love that. It's not a bad little place. Not as nice as this house, but I think you'll like it."

"If you're there, that's all that matters." For the first time she noticed a bruise on his shoulder. It had faded quite a bit, but something heavy must have hit him there to make a grapefruit-size mark. She outlined it gently with her finger. "I've been hanging on to you quite a bit recently. I hope I haven't hurt you."

"Didn't even notice. That bruise is almost gone, anyway."

"How'd you get it?"

"Beam collapsed. Reaction time was too slow."

She swallowed a cry of alarm. After hearing his speech about tough Thunder Mountain guys she figured he wouldn't appreciate that reaction. But the image of him dodging a collapsing beam would probably haunt her for some time. "It could've hit your head."

"But it didn't." He stroked her hip. "That's all that's important."

She looked into his green eyes and shivered at the thought of dangers he faced on a daily basis. "And you're worried about me moving to LA."

"I'm trained to avoid being hurt or killed. You're trained to sing and write music, not navigate your way through a busy urban environment. Logically you'll be performing at night in places where guys could get drunk and disorderly. Instead of taking the elevator to your hotel room, you have to make it back to your apartment without being accosted or followed."

"Ugh. You're making me think of things I hadn't before."

"That's my goal."

"I'll take a self-defense course. I'll figure this out, I promise."

He cupped her chin and stroked his thumb over her

lower lip. "Make friends, get a roommate, travel in groups whenever you can." He grimaced. "Ideally you should have a menacing-looking boyfriend, but I can't bring myself to suggest that."

"I don't want a boyfriend. You've spoiled me for anyone else." She'd meant it as a teasing comment.

Judging from the way he looked at her, he hadn't taken it that way. His eyes shimmered with an emotion that could lead to trouble. "Likewise."

Much more of this and they were liable to say things they couldn't take back. Time to change the mood. She began by massaging his warm chest. "You know what? I think you've developed more muscles since last summer."

He smiled. "Unlikely."

"I think you have. Lie flat and let me take inventory."

"Not gonna argue with that plan." Laughing, he rolled onto his back. "But nothing's changed. I've been doing the same workout at the gym since then. Wait, that's not quite true. When my shifts allow it, I've added some early morning or late evening runs through town. Depending on how many times I go around the square, I probably clock about five miles a day."

"Why did you start doing that?" She swung one leg over his hip so she could start at the top and work her way down over his gorgeous body. By the time she was finished, they'd both be ready to rock and roll. That's what tonight was supposed to be about.

"Nostalgia." He cupped her breasts. "Hey, I want to explore, too."

"Let go, please. You'll get your turn later." Grasping his wrists, she pushed them down to his sides. If he hadn't let her do it she never would have been strong enough, but they'd established the routine last August. All requests were granted without question. "What sort of nostalgia?" She leaned down and kissed the hollow of his throat.

"When I first settled on firefighting as a career, I knew I had to get in shape." He sucked in a breath as she licked her way down to his pecs.

"You've certainly done that." She took his nipple between her teeth and was gratified by his soft groan.

"I used to run on the Forest Service road." He drew in another sharp breath as she swirled her tongue over his warm skin. "Lots of great memories connected with that road. Today we added another one."

"Yeah." She glanced up to discover he'd propped a pillow behind his head so he could watch her progress. "I'll never forget that, Jake."

"Crappy sleigh."

"Didn't matter."

"Nope." His green eyes glittered and his attention drifted to her breasts. "Are you about done? Because if you are, I have some plans for you."

"I'm not even close to done." She returned to the vast erotic territory that was Jake. Besides his impressive pecs, he had a six-pack that could make grown women weep with longing. He might claim that nothing had changed, but she thought his abs had gained more definition since August. She kissed her way across them.

He chuckled. "You're tickling me."

"Then let me move to less ticklish areas." His cock had already risen to the occasion. Although she'd meant to save that for last, she couldn't resist the proud jut of his obvious desire for her. Any girl with access to that primo equipment should be grateful. Grasping the base, she began licking the velvet length of him.

His choked response indicated he hadn't expected that. "I thought…you were going to gradually explore."

"Something caught my attention along the way. Do you mind?"

"Are you kidding? I've spent months dreaming about being in bed with you again, fooling around while we… ah, that's so good."

"How about this?" She closed her mouth over the sensitive tip.

He gasped. "I might lose my mind."

She lifted her head. "Are you saying you want me to stop?"

"God, no."

"That's what I thought." She loved making him come this way. He lost his cool whenever he had sex with her, but oral sex seemed to bring out his most primitive instincts. So she threw herself into it, licking and sucking until he thrashed against the mattress, panting and desperate.

"Tell me what you want," she murmured as she blew against the damp underside of his cock.

He groaned. "Finish this before I go insane."

"I can do that." And she did, pleasuring him until his hips bucked and he erupted. She swallowed all he had to give.

When it was over, he pulled her up so that he could kiss her. Despite everything, he still had the strength for that. "You've said you drop your armor for me," he murmured.

"Because I do." She snuggled against his warm body

and held his gaze as she traced the sculpted line of his cheekbones.

"I've dropped mine, too."

Her heart turned over at the vulnerability revealed by that statement and the trust glowing in his green eyes. "I can tell."

"The feeling's new for me, but I like it."

"Good. It suits you." She kept her tone light, but the conversation tore her apart. He'd offered her a precious gift, one he hadn't possessed years ago. Much as she'd wanted him back then, they wouldn't have been happy together. But now he'd evolved into a man capable of loving her. And the kindest thing she could do was walk away.

11

JAKE HAD EVERY intention of returning the favor Amethyst had granted him, but she snuggled close and talked him out of it. Her argument was perfectly reasonable. The next day she'd be spending Christmas with her folks and he'd be out at the ranch with his foster family. If they didn't sleep for a few hours, they'd both be zombies, not to mention they'd be too worn out to enjoy each other later on.

But curling up with a naked Amethyst and then trying to sleep was more of a challenge than he'd figured on. Although she drifted right off, he lay in the darkness mulling over a couple of nagging problems. Interestingly enough, arousal wasn't the more troublesome of the two. He'd dealt with that before and knew that by focusing on what she needed, namely sleep, he'd reduce the urgency to a manageable level.

Once he'd accomplished that he was free to deal with the second issue. He knew he had to stand by and watch her leave for LA. Yet imagining the terrible things that could happen to her had already driven him crazy and she wasn't even there yet.

A self-defense course was a good idea but not adequate, at least in his view. He started entertaining wild ideas, like going with her. Then what? Would she even let him do that—leave his family and job for her?

Ironically, if she hadn't told him that her sexy persona wasn't the real Amethyst, he might not be as worried. Until she'd admitted that today, he'd thought of her as fearless and bold, even a little intimidating.

Until she'd talked with Chelsea and had become inspired by Finn's migration to Seattle and Matt's struggles in Hollywood, she'd apparently been content to stay in Wyoming and see whether some talent scout found her.

In the meantime she'd put great effort into building a studio in a renovated Victorian that she loved. That implied that she expected to stay awhile. She hadn't been poised for flight. Instead she'd been feathering her nest in Sheridan and making forays around the state to give performances in familiar venues.

While they'd sat having drinks and flirting in the resort's bar last August, she'd described her life. She hadn't sounded frustrated by her lack of fame and fortune. She'd seemed to be having fun while she waited patiently to see whether something more would happen.

What if she was heading to LA because she thought that was the expected thing, the intelligent thing, instead of going because she couldn't help herself? Jake had seen Finn's single-mindedness firsthand. The guy had settled on opening a microbrewery in Seattle and couldn't be dissuaded. Rosie had tried.

Jake hadn't been around when Matt had announced he was leaving to become a Hollywood star, but no doubt the same dynamic had been at work. It sure didn't seem like Amethyst was driven to succeed at that level or she wouldn't be building herself a studio and taking in students. But he didn't think she'd appreciate having him say so. Matter of fact, she'd probably hate it.

Even worse, she might think he'd concocted his theory out of a misguided attempt to keep her safe. He'd always walked a thin line between being protective and overprotective. She'd likely accuse him of crossing it.

So he couldn't talk to her about this. He could only be there for her, love the daylights out of her, and hope that a solution would present itself before she made what could be the biggest mistake of her life.

Exhausted from the intensity of their lovemaking and the hamster wheel his thoughts had been running on, he fell into a restless sleep. Nightmares involving Amethyst being pursued by burly guys through dark streets tortured him until morning light edged through a break in the curtains.

He'd been an early riser ever since he could remember. As a kid seeking refuge in various hidey-holes each night, he'd had to wake up and get out before someone discovered him. The habit of becoming instantly awake at dawn had stuck with him even when he'd tried to break it.

Amethyst had really conked out. He managed to get out of bed without seeing even an eyelash flutter. He was happy to let her sleep. It was bad enough that she might have aches and pains today from all their extra-curricular activity, but at least she'd be a little bit rested.

He hadn't thought that through very well, not this time or back in August. Sending her out on the road last summer after very little sleep could have resulted in a tragedy. When she came to Jackson Hole over New Year's he'd make sure she didn't drive away until she'd had a decent night's rest. Just because he'd learned to function on a few hours in the sack didn't mean he should expect her to.

Once he'd exited the bedroom without waking her, he quietly shut the door. Her razor gave him a halfway decent shave and he went downstairs to get the smoke alarm and his shirt. He put it on to ward off the slight chill in the house but left the tails hanging out.

He started to turn off the Christmas tree lights they'd left on the night before but decided against it because she might enjoy looking at them when she came down. Besides, they were LEDs. With luck he could install the alarm without making a lot of noise. Since he'd be installing it without a power drill that shouldn't be difficult.

She was still snoozing away when he finished, so he went downstairs, made coffee and took a cup into the living room. He wished he had another gift for her that he could tuck under the tree since this was Christmas morning, but he didn't. He sank onto the sofa to drink his coffee and dream of what life could be like if he came back to Sheridan and Amethyst didn't leave. A lot of *ifs* in that dream scenario.

Her bare feet on the stairs made his heart click into high gear. Turning, he watched her come down in her red sleep shirt. Whatever makeup she'd been wearing yesterday was gone and her hair was a tangled mess. He'd never seen a more beautiful woman.

She paused on the bottom step. "Merry Christmas."

"Merry Christmas to you, too." He wanted to go to her and sweep her up in his arms, but he could tell she wasn't quite awake and that might startle her.

"You installed the alarm."

"Tried to be quiet about it."

"You were. I didn't hear a thing. I woke up when I smelled coffee."

He rose. "Come sit and I'll get you some."

"No, you stay there. I'll get my own. I have a package of chocolate doughnuts in the pantry. They're full of preservatives and not the least bit good for us. Want some?"

"Absolutely." He waited until she came back with her coffee and the doughnuts. "Firehouse favorite."

She smiled and sat next to him, her thigh touching his. "My folks cook an elaborate Christmas breakfast, but I like to start with these." She popped open the lid and held out the narrow box.

"Thanks." He took one. "Rosie makes a big breakfast, too, but there's nothing wrong with a few chocolate doughnuts as an appetizer."

"How soon should you be there?"

He glanced at an old-fashioned pendulum clock that hung on the wall. "Soon. Ranch people get up early to feed the animals. But we can have another cup of coffee and a couple more doughnuts before I leave."

"My family won't expect me until a little later." She settled back against the sofa. "Is it terrible of me to wish we didn't have to go somewhere today?"

That comment warmed his heart more than she could know. "If it is, then I'm terrible, too."

"You wouldn't get the holiday feast if you stayed here with me."

He took another doughnut. "What would I get?"

"Tomato soup. Toasted cheese. Lots of sex."

"Sold."

She glanced at him and sighed. "But you drove here so you could hang out with your family for Christmas.

I've always made it a point to be around for Christmas with my folks, and this year it's more important because Sapphire is there and I don't see her all the time like I used to."

"Does she know about your plan to move to LA?" He was trolling for allies and thought Sapphire might be one.

"I'm not sure. She might not have been around when I was discussing it with Chelsea. I'll talk to everybody about it today. Grady's been a few times for gallery openings. He might have some useful info for me."

"He might. Good idea." He wished that some of her contacts had knowledge of the LA entertainment scene. A roommate who was a street-smart woman who'd lived there for years would be an even greater blessing. "You know what? I should go. If I don't, I'll make love to you again, and God knows when we'll leave this house."

That made her laugh. "I hate to admit it, but you're right. I'm sitting here thinking about how many condoms you have left in your jeans' pocket."

"Three, but we're not using them until tonight." Setting down his empty coffee mug, he leaned toward her. "Do we have a plan? What time can you get away?"

She cradled his face in both hands. "You shaved."

"With your razor. Tell me when to show up here because at the moment that's all that I care about, when I'll be able to hold you again."

"Let's say eight. Everything should have wound down by then."

"I'll be here."

"Me, too." Bending toward him, she gave him a soulful kiss that didn't last nearly long enough. "Until then."

"Until then."

She scurried up the stairs. He took their coffee cups into the kitchen, rinsed them and unplugged the pot. Then he walked back into the quiet living room and put on his coat, hat and gloves. He heard the shower come on upstairs and fantasized going up there.

Shaking his head, he discarded the idea. For one thing, he'd probably scare her to death. For another, leaving wouldn't be any easier after he'd made love to her again, so he might as well locate his keys and vamoose.

His keys were AWOL, naturally. When he'd searched the living room, he concluded they were quite likely dangling from the ignition. He'd been out of his ever-lovin' mind last night.

He'd managed to calm down after having a lot of sex and some good conversation. They'd actually slept together for a little while. If he could stay here for the day, they might settle into a less frantic pace. He'd like that.

But she had her obligations and he had his. The word *obligations* didn't fit, though. He loved his family and she obviously loved hers, so there was no resentment involved, only sadness that they couldn't be together.

Despite feeling bonded with her, he wasn't on track to become a permanent part of her life. Climbing into his very cold truck, he started the engine and the music came on. He sat there listening to her sing to him and fought the urge to go back in there. Damn it, leaving her seemed wrong. But he pulled out of her drive and drove away.

His funky mood lasted until he turned onto the ranch road. The hand-carved hanging sign for Thunder Mountain Academy always gave him a lift. Damon and Phil had made it with some design advice from their saddle maker friend Ben Radcliffe. Rosie had decorated the sign with a fresh pine wreath.

Yeah, he needed to be here today with the two people who'd literally saved his life. At the time he'd been hiding out in vacant houses and storage sheds every night. He hadn't realized how dangerous it was.

When he pulled into the circular drive in front of the ranch house, the Christmas lights were all on. He wouldn't have been able to see that if the sun had been shining, but heavy clouds had moved in. He vaguely remembered that someone had mentioned snow in the forecast.

Herb and Rosie would have a big electric bill but not as big as it could have been if he hadn't arrived in the nick of time. He pictured himself moving back to Sheridan and supervising the Christmas lights project every year. Right there was another excellent reason to check into job openings. He might drive over to the fire department tomorrow morning before he left town.

As he climbed out of the truck he took a deep breath and savored wood smoke combined with cinnamon rolls baking and bacon frying. Christmas morning at Thunder Mountain Ranch. Rosie and Herb would have been up for a couple of hours already, but Rosie always delayed Christmas morning breakfast until after the chores were done. That way everyone could sit around the table, drink coffee and have an extra cinnamon roll instead of rushing off to feed and water.

He spotted a car he didn't recognize and wondered who was joining them for Christmas breakfast.

About that time Cade came out onto the front porch, a mug of coffee in one hand. He was wearing a sheepskin vest that looked new. "Thought I heard you drive up! Was a little worried you'd bail on us this morning. Having other activities on your schedule and all."

"Wouldn't miss it."

Cade grinned. "I'm guessing she kicked you out 'cause she had better things to do today."

"Something like that." Jake climbed the steps. "Nice vest."

"Christmas present from the in-laws, or soon to be in-laws. They came for breakfast. Lexi was afraid to let 'em come last night because that would have tipped me off for sure."

"So that's who the car belongs to."

"Yep. Listen, we need to get inside before I freeze my tokus, but is everything okay?"

"So far."

"Still just fun and games, right?"

Jake hesitated a beat too long.

"Oh, buddy, you don't want to fall for her. That's a heartache waiting to happen."

"Probably, but I'll see it through."

"I hate hearing you say that. Even Mom thinks she's not right for you."

"That's because she doesn't know Amethyst like I do."

"Well, I should hope not!" Cade slapped him on the back. "Come in and have some chow. Then we'll shoot some pool while I talk you out of this self-destructive path you're heading down."

Jake followed him into the house. Cade was right that falling for Amethyst would likely put him in a world of hurt. But it was too late now.

12

AFTER GOING THROUGH the opening of presents and an elaborate brunch with no mention of the LA move, Amethyst concluded that Sapphire and Grady hadn't heard about it at the party the night before and therefore hadn't mentioned it to her parents. She took a deep breath. "Since we're all here, it's the perfect time for me to announce my plan for the New Year. I've decided to move to LA."

She was greeted with stunned silence. "Surely it's not a surprise," she said. "I've been rattling around in Wyoming and no talent scout has shown up. I've sent out demos but nobody's come knocking on my door. After talking with Chelsea yesterday—she's Finn O'Roarke's fiancée and a marketing whiz—I decided to become more proactive."

"Wow." Sapphire was the first one to speak. "I guess it's not a total surprise, but I thought you'd decided to stay here where the cost of living was cheaper until you'd made something happen."

"That was the plan, but I'm convinced I can't make something happen from here. I might have an amazing stroke of luck and be discovered at some Wyoming venue, but it hasn't happened yet and I've been doing this for three-plus years."

"It's a very exciting idea." Her mother's tone was cautious. "You know how much I believe in you."

"Same here," her father said. He normally wore black turtlenecks and jeans but in honor of Christmas he'd added a sweatshirt with Santa playing a sax. "You have a boatload of talent. The competition's tough over there, but you can handle it. You'll knock 'em dead."

"Thanks, Dad."

"You will for sure." Her mom looked especially regal in a dark green outfit that had been a gift from Sapphire. "I'm not the least bit worried about that. I'm thinking of the stuff moms always imagine, like whether you'll get mixed up on the freeway and wind up in a terrible neighborhood, or whether you'll move in next door to a drug dealer."

Amethyst laughed. "Oh, Mom. Have a little faith. You sound just like—" She caught herself before saying his name. "A typical mom. I'll be fine." She avoided looking at Sapphire who'd probably known whose name she'd bleeped out.

"And I'm a typical dad," her father said. "Do you have any friends over there? People you went to college with?"

"Not really, but—"

"Wait!" Her mother sat forward. "There's what's-his-name, the one who went over to become a big star a couple of years ago."

"Matt Forrest."

"Right. I talked to Rosie last month in the grocery store and he was still there trying to make it. You could get his contact info."

"I will, but from what I hear, he might be on location for the next few months. Besides, I'll make friends. No worries."

Sapphire looked over at Grady. "You've been to LA several times for gallery shows. Any advice for my big sister?"

"You know, this is so not my area." He gazed at Amethyst. "I totally agree with the logic of making this move, but I'm a Wyoming boy. If living in LA was the only way I could make it with my art…" He shook his head. "I'm not sure what I'd do. City life is not for me. It may turn out that you love it, though."

"I don't know if I will or not. But if I expect to make any progress in my career, I need to give it a shot."

"I'll bet Matt's made some good friends while he's been living there," her mom said. "Even if he won't be around, his friends could be of some help."

Amethyst smiled at her. "I'll contact him. If he offers his friends' help, then I'll consider it, but I don't want to give him the impression I need babysitting. Anyone who's trying to make it in the recording business needs to be able to stand on their own two feet."

"I'll go over with you for a week or so," Sapphire said. "Just until you're settled."

She was tempted but that would be selfish. "Thank you, but I can't let you do that."

Sapphire lifted her chin. "Try and stop me. I'm going."

"I like that plan," her mother said. "The two of you are a force to be reckoned with. I'd feel much better if you spent that first week there, Sapphire. Maybe two weeks."

"I can't accept it." Amethyst held her sister's gaze.

"It's a lovely offer, Sapphire, but you don't have enough time to plan your own wedding let alone spend a week or two making sure I don't move in next to a drug dealer."

"But—"

"Give it up, sis. I really won't let you go over there with me."

Sapphire rolled her eyes and sighed. "Okay, I won't force myself on you, but if you change your mind…"

"I won't. This is my plan and I'm not going to inconvenience other people in order to make it happen."

"As long as I don't have any gigs scheduled," her dad said, "it wouldn't be an inconvenience for me. I set my own schedule."

"I'm not letting any of you interrupt your lives." She glanced around the table. "I appreciate your generous offers, but I can't predict exactly when the move might take place so it's best if I don't get anyone else involved. I'll need to sublet my half of the house and that could be a last-minute arrangement. Once I find the right person, I could be gone within forty-eight hours. I'll need to stay extremely flexible."

Her mother and father exchanged a look. She'd seen it a thousand times. It meant they would drop the subject for now but it was by no means forgotten.

Sure enough, her dad challenged her to a game of chess that afternoon. They often played on Christmas, so that wasn't unusual. He'd taught both her and Sapphire but she'd been the only one who'd kept up with it. Still, she suspected he had ulterior motives for wanting some time with her.

They were well into the game, which they'd set up in front of the fire, when he broached the subject. "I'm not saying you shouldn't go to LA." He captured a pawn.

"But you seem to have made the decision based on what Finn's fiancée said. How well do you know her?"

"We just met. Judging from what everyone says, she's largely responsible for Finn's success with his microbrewery. Her mention of LA was very casual, but something clicked for me. I knew it was what I should do." She moved her knight. "Check."

"Nice job." He maneuvered out of the tight spot she'd put him in. "So this is something you think you *should* do?"

"Bad choice of words. I meant it's something I *want* to do."

"I hope so, because when it comes to anything creative, the word *should* doesn't work well at all."

"You're right."

"I keep thinking of that music prof you liked so much. What was his name?"

"Professor Edenbury." If she could pull this off and actually get a recording contract, he was one of the first people she'd tell once she'd notified her family.

Her father hesitated, his hand poised over the board. "Do his expectations have anything to do with this?"

"Now that would be silly, wouldn't it? He may not even remember me."

"Oh, I'm sure he does. He had big plans for you."

"Well, I'm not doing this for Professor Edenbury, Dad. I'm doing it for me. By the way, did you and your jazz buddies ever talk about going over there and trying your luck? Before you met Mom, of course."

"Sure we did." He made his move. "Check."

"Oh, good one." But she'd anticipated it and weaseled out of his trap. "So why didn't you?"

"Great question, Amie." He'd shortened both his

daughters' names because he was a nickname kind of guy. Her mother hadn't been pleased, but he'd stuck to his guns on the matter. "One night after a gig the four of us got moderately toasted."

She smiled. "Only moderately?"

That made him laugh. "That night, yeah, because once we got on the subject, we knew if we were going to do it, we needed to hop in the car right then and drive to California. We were young and unattached. We could live on the beach if we had to."

"Did you go?"

"No. We argued the question six ways to Sunday and we didn't come to a conclusion until after four in the morning. We'd listed every pro and con we could think of and we went through several six-packs and bags of Cheetos."

She gazed at him, the game forgotten, as she imagined her father as a young man hanging out with his buddies and deciding their future. "Why did you decide to stay?"

"Because we all agreed we loved this silly place called Wyoming. We might never be rich and famous, but we'd have mountains to look at and minimal traffic. Country living was in our blood and we didn't want to give it up. Then I met your mother and knew I'd made the right choice. When you came along, and later Sapphie, I really knew it."

"That's a great story. Any regrets?"

"Not a one. Staying local and playing gigs here and there has worked for me. But I'm not suggesting it would work for you. I just hope you give the decision the same amount of attention that my buddies and I did that night. Checkmate."

She looked at the board and realized he had her beat. She glanced up. "You win, Dad."

"Considering I have you, Sapphie and your mom, I can't lose."

JAKE RESISTED THE urge to text Amethyst during the day although he desperately wanted to know how her family had reacted to news of the move to LA. Surely he wasn't the only one who was worried. He turned his sound off but he checked the screen every once in a while to see if she'd sent him a message.

But when Cade announced the traditional Christmas snowball fight was about to commence, Jake left his phone on the kitchen counter. Grabbing his coat and gloves, he headed outside, eager to work off some tension.

Although Thunder Mountain's foster care program had ended quite a while ago, the temporary financial crisis Rosie and Herb had endured recently had brought many of the brothers back to Sheridan. They'd helped set up Thunder Mountain Academy to make the ranch solvent again and they'd reinstituted many of the nostalgic activities Jake had cherished as a teenager. The Christmas Day snowball fight was one of them.

In the old days it had been all guys manning the barricades, but times had changed. Lexi and Chelsea wanted in on it and Phil vowed she'd be on the front lines next year assuming she could talk Rosie into holding her kid. Rosie promised she would.

Chelsea and Lexi wanted to be on the opposite team from their fiancés, so Jake volunteered to join them and face off against Cade, Damon and Finn. After listening to the women outline their battle plan, Jake figured it would be at least an even fight, and his team might actually win. The women were focused while Cade's team spent the preparation time joking around and acting macho.

While Cade and Damon wasted precious minutes arguing about the correct way to build a fort, Jake's team worked smoothly to create a sturdy barrier with an impressive stockpile of ammunition. As Jake crouched in the middle between the two women, he took inventory of their skills. "Either of you play softball?"

"Was on the state championship squad," Chelsea said.

"Me, too." Lexi exchanged a high five with Chelsea.

Jake hunkered down. "We're going to whip their butts."

The fight didn't last very long because Cade's team ran out of premade snowballs and Jake's crew charged their flimsy barricade armed to the teeth. Lexi's parents, along with Phil, Rosie and Herb sat on the porch scoring the hits. Jake assumed that trampling over the other team's fort pretty much gave his team the win, but tradition meant leaving it up to the judges on the porch.

They all voted for Jake's team. Laughing, he hugged his teammates.

"Foul!" Cade cried. "The judges were prejudiced!"

"No," Phil said, "you three were treating this like a slam dunk you couldn't lose, and the opposing team took advantage of your overconfidence. We stand by our decision." She turned to Rosie. "Am I right?"

"Yes, ma'am." Rosie gave her a big smile.

"All righty, then." Cade abandoned his protest. "Drinks for all! Except Phil, who's on the wagon until she drops that kid."

"Don't remind me." Phil linked her arm through Damon's as they filed into the house. "Good thing I'm excited about this baby because our decision to have her has seriously impacted my life."

Jake took note of that comment. He'd never considered the sacrifices required of a pregnant woman, but Phil was making it very real. Amethyst might never want marriage, let alone a baby. He hadn't thought much about the concept of having kids. His childhood had been traumatic and he couldn't imagine bringing an infant into the world until he had a stable relationship with a woman who wanted the same things he did.

On the surface, that woman wasn't Amethyst. If he took her at her word, she'd be overjoyed to live in LA and be a star with hit songs and regular concert tours. Yet spending the night in the cozy Victorian had given him a glimpse of a life that seemed at odds with that scenario.

After the snowball fight he found himself momentarily alone with Chelsea in the kitchen when she went to fetch a cup of coffee and he wanted to retrieve his phone. He picked it up and shoved it in his pocket. He couldn't have asked for a better opportunity to talk with Chelsea so he'd check his phone later. "It looks as if Amethyst really is moving to LA."

"Good for her." Chelsea poured her coffee into a mug. "Although I admit I was surprised at how quickly she jumped on the idea after my casual remark yesterday."

"She respects your expertise."

"I'm no expert in this area, but it makes sense to me that if she wants a recording contract she'll do better if she can meet with people face-to-face."

Jake hesitated as he considered how to approach the issue. "She'd hoped that a talent scout would discover her in Wyoming."

"She told me that. But waiting for success to come to you isn't a very good strategy."

"No." Jake could tell she was ready to head back out to the porch. "Before you go, let me ask you something."

"Sure." She paused and leaned against the counter.

"What if she only thinks she wants this? What if everyone's been telling her she has a shot and now she feels as if it's put up or shut up time?"

"In other words, she might have the talent but not the drive?"

"Right. Waiting for a talent scout to show up doesn't sound like someone who'll do whatever's necessary to make a dream come true."

"No, it doesn't." Chelsea's gaze was sympathetic. "You really care about her."

"I do. And I'm worried."

"Let me think." Putting down her coffee, she paced the length of the kitchen while she ruffled her damp hair, making the multicolored strands dance around. Finally she turned to him. "I'm guessing you'd like me to talk to her, maybe invite her for coffee before Finn and I leave town."

"Would you?" A ray of hope pierced the gloom.

"I would if I thought it would help. But it won't. She's announced to everyone she's moving to LA. How do you suppose she'd react if I tried to convince her not to go because she's missing that fire in the belly?"

"She'd say you're wrong, that you don't know her well enough and she's highly motivated."

"Exactly. No way would she listen carefully and then admit that I'm right. Unfortunately this isn't something I can tell her. You obviously know her better than I do, but I question whether you or anyone can tell her without creating an explosion. You'll come off as someone who doesn't believe in her."

He groaned. "I believe in her. She's amazing. But she's *happy* here. You should see the studio she's set up in her house. She loves giving voice lessons to little kids. What if she tears her life apart and it doesn't work out? Or even worse, what if it does work out and it's not what she wants, after all?"

"Then she'll suffer and you'll go through hell knowing she's made a terrible mistake. You'll ask yourself if you could have prevented it, even though you understand intellectually that people have to learn for themselves. It's no fun watching someone you love barreling down the tracks toward a potential train wreck. Believe me, I know."

"Who did you go through it with?"

"Finn."

"Finn?" Jake stared at her. "I thought you two met, fell in love and got engaged. Nobody mentioned any train wreck."

"Then I guess you didn't hear about his first marriage."

He thought back. "You know, I vaguely remember something like that, but I was in Jackson Hole by then and didn't get home much. What happened?"

"We had chemistry from the day we met but he was afraid I'd tempt him to ignore his business obligations. So he married someone else, someone who didn't have the power to distract him."

"Wow, I gave him credit for being a lot smarter."

"It was an emotional decision. He was afraid to do the wrong thing so he did something worse. If I'd tried to tell him, he wouldn't have listened. I doubt Amethyst will listen to you, either, even if you have the purest of intentions."

"Which I don't." He sighed. "I'm thinking of her, but I'm also thinking of myself. Tomorrow I'm planning to check for openings at the fire department here. I want to move back."

"Because of her?"

"No. That much is clear in my head. I want to live here again whether she goes or stays."

"Does she know you're moving back to Sheridan?"

He shook his head. "I thought it would complicate things."

"You could try mentioning it. At least then she'd have all the facts before she heads off to LA."

"I don't know. She might think I'm doing it in hopes she'll stay."

"Just tell her the truth. Once you have a job, you're moving back regardless of what she does. You can't control what she chooses to believe. But when she's balancing what she hopes to find in LA against what she's giving up here, you'll be included in her calculations. You never know. That might tip the scales."

"I'll think about it." He gave her a weary smile. "Thanks for the heart-to-heart."

"Sorry I don't have a magic solution."

"Yeah, I was hoping you would, but you're right. There isn't one."

When she left the kitchen he stayed behind and pulled out his phone. His pulse jumped when he saw the text from Amethyst: Change of plans. Mom and Dad want us all to go caroling at 5 and dinner here afterward. You're invited.

13

AMETHYST THOUGHT CURIOSITY was at the bottom of her mother's caroling and dinner plan. Maybe she'd noticed her daughter checking her phone several times during the day and had figured out that Jake Ramsey was back in the picture. Getting him under the Ferguson family roof and at their dinner table was a time-honored way to confirm those suspicions.

That was fine with Amethyst. She wasn't deliberately keeping Jake a secret, but they weren't heading for a fairy-tale ending so there seemed to be no reason to include him in her family's plans. Her mother obviously felt differently.

Jake arrived looking more gorgeous than any man had a right to be. He was freshly shaved, but then, he would be. He knew what was scheduled after the family togetherness time.

Her mother suggested that Jake should leave on his coat and hat because everyone else could be ready in a jiffy. Amethyst couldn't blame her mother for not wanting to alter the picture he made standing in their entry hall. He'd turned up the collar of his sheepskin coat against the night air and his perfectly creased gray Stetson, snug jeans and polished boots made him look like an ad for Western wear. Once again she was amazed that the single women of Jackson Hole hadn't lined up outside the firehouse.

Because he was ready to go, he was free to help her with her coat and he managed it with polite chivalry as if they were only good friends and not passionate lovers. He charmed her parents with his winning smile and thanked them for inviting him. He called them Mr. and Mrs. Ferguson because that had been protocol when he'd dated her ten years ago.

Her mother asked him to use Jane and Stan instead, and he slipped right into that without awkwardness or hesitation. Amethyst couldn't help contrasting the self-confident person he was now with the high school senior who'd been so unsure of his place in the world. His work as a firefighter had given him an impressive physique, but it had also matured him. He appeared completely relaxed, as if he didn't consider it the least bit strange that he'd received a last-minute invitation to join a family Christmas activity.

At one point Amethyst's mother glanced over and lifted her eyebrows as if silently asking why her daughter didn't snap up this paragon. That gesture was enough to convince Amethyst why her mom had issued the invitation. She hadn't said much since breakfast about the LA plan. She must be frustrated that her teaching job at the high school would keep her from checking on the safety of Amethyst's apartment until at least spring break. She probably hoped that a romance with Jake would postpone the move or maybe even cancel it.

Neither of her parents could be blamed for their nervousness about LA. She wasn't entirely calm herself. But that didn't mean she wasn't going.

"I should warn you that I'm not much of a singer." Jake glanced at Amethyst's parents. "I hope the rest of you will be really loud so nobody can hear me."

Her mother patted his arm. "I'm not much of a singer, either, Jake. I count on Amethyst and Stan to help me stay on pitch. Sapphire can hold her own, but I've never heard Grady sing."

"I have." Jake grinned at his foster brother. "He's got a halfway decent voice but—"

"Hey!" Grady threw back his shoulders. "I have a fully decent voice. There's nothing halfway about it."

"You know, that's a fact." Jake tugged his Stetson a little lower. "Now if you could only remember the words, you'd be all set. If anyone hears a person going 'Silent night, holy night, something something, something something,' that will be Grady."

"Not anymore." Grady whipped out his phone. "Times have changed, bro. Thanks to the modern age, I have the words at my fingertips."

Jake pointed to Grady's thick gloves. "Those don't look like the kind for handling a phone. In essence you have no fingertips."

"Oh. Yeah, that's true." He pocketed his cell. "Didn't think of that. Guess I'm back to mumbling."

"Never fear. I've got you covered." Amethyst's father held up a sheaf of papers. "When we came up with this idea, I printed out a few carols." He passed them out. "Here's the plan. We walk to the end of the block. Jane and I will take the lead and you four will follow. At the end of the block we'll cross the street and serenade the people who bought the Blakely's house. It's a young couple with a baby. I've met them and they seem nice. Then we'll cross back to Mrs. Gentry's."

"Does she still live there?" Sapphire asked.

He nodded. "Yes, but she's at least ninety and she's hard of hearing so we'll have to belt out those tunes. Anyway, we'll crisscross the street and end up back here for dinner. Everybody ready?"

"Ready as we'll ever be," Amethyst said.

"Then let's go surprise the neighbors."

"Surprise them?" Jake asked. "This isn't a family tradition?"

"Used to be," her dad said. "Back when we could corral the girls and bribe them with promises of hot cocoa and Christmas cookies afterward. Then the day came when they flatly refused, regardless of the bribe."

"Because it was embarrassing, Dad," Sapphire said as they headed out the door. "Nobody else did it and we had friends living around here. We'd hear about it when we got back from Christmas vacation. They called us the Trapp Family Singers. It was not cool."

"And none of our neighbors knew how to react." Amethyst suspected it would be even more confusing to them this year after a thirteen-year hiatus. "They weren't sure whether to invite us in for dinner, give us money or bring out a platter of Christmas cookies."

"No kidding," Sapphire said. "They were completely bewildered. Mrs. Lester wanted to give us the poinsettia she had sitting in her entry."

Amethyst started laughing. "Yeah, and you almost took it until Mom made you put it back. Oh, and remember the Danforths and the bowl of candy?"

"The candy they started throwing at us like they were on a parade float?" Sapphire rolled her eyes. "But that was better than Mr. Johannsen trying to make us eat some *surstromming*."

"Eeuuww, yes! That was gross!" Amethyst could still remember the smell of the fermented fish.

"Hey, Dad," Sapphire called out. "Could we skip his house? Just in case he still eats that awful stuff?"

"He's moved," their father said over his shoulder, "so you don't have to worry about it."

"That's a relief." Sapphire motioned Amethyst and Jake to the back of the parade. "You two bring up the rear." She lowered her voice. "I'm sure you have things to talk about."

"Um, okay." Amethyst glanced at Jake. "Sorry about this," she murmured.

"No problem." He took her hand. "I can't wait to see how this caroling gig turns out. I'm a little sorry Mr. Johannsen moved away."

"Trust me, you would not want to get anywhere near that stuff. But thanks for accepting the invitation." She glanced over at him. "Did I pull you away from anything important at the ranch?"

"Not really. Playing poker and pool, watching basketball, eating leftovers. They all thought it was hysterical that I was coming here to go caroling."

"I'm guessing you've never done it before."

"Good guess. But it seems kind of nice, growing up in a neighborhood where you knew most of the people."

"You probably didn't have much to do with the neighbors when you lived with your dad."

"Sure didn't. He was the most antisocial person I've ever known and if I talked to anybody who lived around there I was in big trouble."

"I never asked you before, but do you know where he is?"

"No, which is fine with me. Rosie used her connections in social services to keep tabs on him for a while. I was petrified that he'd try to take me away from the ranch. Then he left town, thank God. Never heard from him again."

"Good."

"Yeah, really. I have my family, now, and they're great." He glanced around. "This is nice, though, walking along looking at all the Christmas lights. We didn't get to do that when we were dating."

"Nope. That's what happens when you break up right before Christmas."

"There should be a rule—no breakups right before Christmas. That was one of my worst holidays ever."

"Mine, too."

He squeezed her hand. "Sorry. Entirely my fault. I promise not to go stomping off like that in the next twelve hours so we should be okay this Christmas."

"Good to know." She tugged on his hand so he'd slow down. "I should probably warn you that my parents aren't completely in favor of my going to LA and I think they're hoping you'll be a factor in changing my mind."

"Which is why I got the sudden invitation, right?"

"Yes."

"I kind of figured that. And I need to tell you something in case it comes up in conversation. I'm going to see if I can get on with the fire department here."

She sucked in a breath. "Because you're hoping I'll change my mind, too?"

"No, not at all. Whether you leave or stay, I'm still

doing it. If you change your mind and decide to stick around, that would be wonderful, but that's not the deciding factor."

She probed his statement for any hidden agenda and didn't find one. He'd never lied to her, so she was inclined to believe him. "So what is the deciding factor?"

"Simple. I'm homesick. Rosie and Herb are the only parents I have, and I want to be able to see them on a regular basis. I didn't realize how much I'd missed the ranch and being with them until I came back this Christmas. Cade and Damon have moved back, too, so I can hang out with them. When others visit, I'll be around."

"You'd live at the ranch?"

"No, that's not practical. The Academy students are staying in the cabins now, except for vacations, and I don't want to move into one of Rosie and Herb's guest rooms. I'm too used to being on my own. Besides, a place close to the station makes more sense."

"My house isn't that far from the station." She wasn't sure how she felt about him living in the space, but at least he could be trusted not to trash her studio.

"That's true."

"My half of the rent's reasonable."

"You think I should take over your lease?" He sounded surprised.

"I don't know. Arlene might freak out if I said a guy was moving in. Or she might like it from a security standpoint, although we don't have much in the way of crime around there. I'd have to ask her."

"I love that house, but there may not be a job opening for me. I'm going to check on that in the morning before I leave town, but I won't move until I have something lined up."

"Tell you what, I won't go looking for someone to sublet it until you find out about the job."

"Thanks. The idea's growing on me." He took a deep breath. "Although moving in there after you're gone would be...a little weird."

"I'm sure. Knowing you were moving in would be weird for me, too. But I'd love it if I didn't have to tear out my studio."

"But why would you want to keep it if you're never going to use it again? You could take some of the equipment to LA and sell the rest, which would give you extra money."

She thought about it and knew he was right. If she sublet her space to anyone besides Jake, they'd expect her to dismantle the studio. Finding a musician to move in was unlikely, and it would have to be the right musician, someone who'd treat the studio with respect. She should take it apart and sell what she couldn't use. The soundproofing she'd done would be wasted, but moving on meant sacrifice.

"If I ended up renting from you, I'd let you take everything out gradually," he said. "That way you wouldn't have to rush to strip it all away. That could be stressful."

"It could, and I appreciate the offer. But I'm a rip-off-the-bandage kind of girl, so if that studio is destined to go, then I might as well get it over with."

They walked in silence for a little longer.

"You know, on second thought," he said, "what if you left everything the way it is? I don't need that second bedroom for anything. You could rent a furnished apartment until you see how it all goes. Then you'd only have to take your clothes and what few other things you'd need."

"You mean leave all my furniture, too?"

"Sure. Or I could buy it from you if you want. It's nicer than what I have. That way you don't have the hassle of renting a truck and hauling furniture into your new apartment."

"It would be a heck of a lot easier, wouldn't it?"

"Seems like it to me."

"Let me think about it. First, you have to get a job with the fire department."

"If they have an opening, you could pack up and leave whenever you want."

"I could." Her stomach began to churn with a combination of excitement and anxiety. If Jake's visit to the fire department in the morning produced a job, she was free to simply take off. Then she remembered her New Year's Eve gig and was relieved that she couldn't go immediately even if Jake did get hired right away. She wanted to go to LA. She really did. But leaving next week seemed a little hasty.

"I couldn't go until after New Year's," she said. "I agreed to perform in Jackson Hole and canceling at this late date would be unprofessional."

"You're right. You can't cancel now. Anyway, I'm selfish enough to want to see you again before you take off."

She squeezed his hand. "I want that, too. And, by the way, I appreciate this gesture on your part."

"It might not work. It all hinges on the job situation."

"I know, but you're still attempting to help me get there even though you don't think it's a great idea. Or have you changed your mind?"

"Not really. But if that's what you want, then you need to give it a shot."

"Thank you. That means so much to me."

"Okay, troops!" her dad called out. "Time to cross the street. Watch for cars."

"There aren't any cars, Dad," Sapphire said.

Her father laughed. "Sorry. Force of habit."

Amethyst's heart swelled with affection as she thought of all the times her parents had cautioned her and her sister to watch out for this and that. No wonder they were worried about this move. They couldn't be expected to simply turn off that impulse, no matter how old she was.

Once they were all on the other side of the street in front of what used to be the Blakely house, her dad arranged them in a semicircle. Then he gave out the stapled sets of lyrics and hummed the opening note of "Joy to the World." Jake fumbled with the pages and finally let go of her hand so he could deal with them.

As the six of them launched into the carol, she discovered that Jake wasn't such a bad singer. His deep baritone was untrained but he had a good ear and stayed on pitch. This was going to be fun, after all.

They were partway through the song when the door opened and a woman and a man came out wearing their coats. The woman held a blanket-wrapped bundle that was probably the baby swaddled against the cold. A second woman with long blond hair stepped onto the porch and closed the door behind her. She hugged a furry coat to her body instead of fastening it and she kept looking at Jake.

Amethyst couldn't blame her. He was gorgeous. She'd been spoiled the past couple of days because she hadn't had to deal with watching attractive women ogle Jake. This one was subtle about it, but she clearly found him appealing. Well, she was out of luck, at least for the time being.

When the carol ended, the women both applauded and the blonde called out, "Jake, is that you?"

Amethyst's jaw tightened. Damn.

Jake hesitated a moment. "Marla?"

"It's me! I've moved to Sheridan!" She made her way down the porch steps toward Jake. "It's so good to see you. I thought we'd lost touch forever. Are you back in town, too?"

"Not permanently yet, but I hope to be soon. Let me introduce you to my friends."

Friends. Amethyst winced at the casual term that didn't come close to describing how she felt about Jake and how she believed he felt about her. But, under the circumstances, she couldn't claim to be anything else.

14

TALK ABOUT ROTTEN TIMING. But he couldn't introduce Amethyst as his girlfriend because she wasn't. He knew she wasn't happy about the chance meeting with an old flame, but then, neither was he. On the other hand, he didn't want to be rude to Marla. They'd had a good thing going for a while.

At the time he'd taken the job in Jackson Hole, she'd been immersed in her accounting courses. She'd made a couple of trips to Jackson during breaks in her schedule and he'd made a couple to Sheridan, but in the end the relationship hadn't survived the separation. She'd sent him a wedding invitation to a ceremony down in Cheyenne two years ago but she wasn't acting married now.

She didn't specifically mention a divorce, but when they all tromped up to the porch to meet her sister, brother-in-law and the baby, Marla said she'd moved to Sheridan to be with them. Her brother-in-law worked for the bank and had recommended her for a job.

While everyone goo-gooed at the baby, Marla asked for his cell number so she could text him hers. He couldn't figure out any way to refuse. It wasn't as if he had a commitment to someone else. He was sure Amethyst had heard the entire exchange, damn it.

He wasn't interested in Marla. He wanted Amethyst, but she might eventually be lost to him. He didn't intend to stay celibate for the rest of his life and mourn the loss of his one true love, so if the time came when he had to accept that Amethyst would never be with him, he'd take comfort elsewhere. If Marla was still available, well… he might take comfort with her.

Amethyst had probably figured all that out. Women were quick to do that. He had a strong feeling the subject would come up once they were alone, but Amethyst was a fair person. She'd know that she didn't have a leg to stand on. That didn't mean she had to like this turn of events. In a way, he found her irritation encouraging.

Other promising signs had cropped up tonight. He was serious about renting her half of the Victorian if he got a job, but he had ulterior motives. So far she hadn't called him on it, but she was smart so she might before too long.

If he was right that she was ambivalent about the move, having the chance to accomplish it right away with a minimum of fuss might be startling enough to make her question her decision. If that backfired and she hightailed it over to LA thanks to his help, then coming home would be really easy if it didn't work out for her.

He wanted a job in Sheridan for many reasons, but securing the Victorian and keeping it ready for Amethyst's possible return was now high on his list. She'd guess his motives at some point and he'd be happy to confess if she did. He hoped that eventually she'd want to come back to the house and to him, but if not, he'd live with the memories they'd shared for as long as he could stand it.

Finally the carolers extricated themselves from the very nice couple, their sweet baby and a woman Jake had not expected to deal with tonight. They all crossed the street to Mrs. Gentry's, the lady Stan had said was going deaf.

Jake had never had a grandparent in his life and he thought that was sad because he'd be an excellent grandson. He'd check on them to see if they needed anything and be tolerant of their infirmities. Maybe being a foster kid without the normal advantages had contributed to his tenderness toward older people. When a person had experienced being at a disadvantage, they understood how it felt.

Because of that, he suggested ringing the doorbell before they started singing. Rosie had once told him that people who lived alone and were hard of hearing often increased the volume on their doorbell chime and their telephone ring. Jake had taken a personal interest in providing Mrs. Gentry with a Christmas carol tonight.

In fact, he stayed at the door until she came in response to the doorbell. He glanced down at a plump little lady with wispy white curls framing her round, pink-cheeked face. She wore a Frosty the Snowman sweatshirt, gray sweatpants and bunny slippers.

He smiled and touched the brim of his hat. "Merry Christmas, Mrs. Gentry!"

She shouted right back at him. "Merry Christmas to you, cutie-pie! Looks like you're here with the Fergusons! What can I do for you?"

"We want to sing you a Christmas carol!"

"Wonderful!" She clapped her hands.

"Want to bundle up so you can come out and enjoy it?"

"Of course! Whatcha gonna sing?"

"What's your favorite?" He hoped Stan had included it in the mix.

"'Grandma Got Run Over by a Reindeer.' I'll get my wrap!"

Jake turned back to Stan, who was cracking up. "Do you know it?"

"Not all of it. You had to ask, didn't you?"

"No worries." Jake grinned as he returned to the group. "I know it. We used to drive Herb and Rosie crazy with that song. I'll bet even Grady knows most of the words."

Grady nodded. "Yep, sure do."

"So do we." Amethyst exchanged a smile with her sister.

"Then you four take the lead." Stan glanced at his wife. "The old folks will mumble along."

"You can mumble if you want," Jane said. "I know the words. Sapphire and Amethyst drove *me* crazy singing it."

Stan looked confused. "I don't remember that. Where was I?"

"Traveling the state doing Christmas shows," she said gently. "We needed the money a lot more back then."

"Guess I've sort of blocked those years."

"Here I am!" Mrs. Gentry came out to the porch and closed the door behind her. She was still wearing her bunny slippers but she'd added a bright red parka and a Santa hat. "Sing away!"

Jake turned to Amethyst. "You're the professional. You'd better start us off."

"Okay." She hummed the opening note. "On three. One, two..."

And they were off, everybody except Stan belting

out a song about poor Grandma's fatal encounter. Stan jumped in each time they reached the chorus, and Mrs. Gentry sang it all at the top of her lungs while she danced a jig on her porch. Hysterical as that was to watch, Jake hoped she didn't slip on an icy patch and fall down.

Fortunately she didn't. When they were finished she insisted everyone had to come in for a mug of hard cider that she guaranteed would put hair on their chests. Jake immediately accepted, which meant everyone else had to go along, but judging from the laughter and smiles, he didn't think they minded.

Mrs. Gentry's artificial tree was loaded with delicate-looking ornaments and large clumps of tinsel. Jake steered clear of it but even so the tinsel shivered as he went by. Christmas-themed knickknacks covered every available surface and Jake moved carefully as he helped Amethyst with her coat and took off his own. One wrong move and he could take out an entire nativity scene.

Jane offered to help with the cider but Mrs. Gentry told her to find a seat and get comfortable. The men hung the coats on a wooden coat tree that already held Mrs. Gentry's red parka although she'd left on the Santa hat. Keeping the coat tree from falling under the load took some balancing, but they managed it while they waited for the women to sit.

When Jake turned around, all three ladies were in a row on the sofa. That left a recliner, probably Mrs. Gentry's spot since it faced the TV, and two dainty armchairs with seats that had flowers stitched on the seat cushions.

Jake wasn't going to take the recliner and he was afraid he'd break those chairs, plus, there were only two. "You guys go ahead." He gestured toward the chairs. "I'll stand."

Grady shook his head. "I'm not taking a chance on one of those."

"Oh, for goodness' sake." Jane moved over to one of the chairs. "Stan, you take the other one. It'll hold you. Your mother had some just like this."

Sapphire scooted to one end of the sofa. "We can fit both of you guys on here with us."

"Definitely." Amethyst moved to the other end.

Grady and Jake looked at each other, shrugged and wedged themselves in between the women.

"I won't be able to drink cider." Grady began to chuckle.

"Why not?" Sapphire glanced at him. "You're not driving anywhere."

"I can't move my arms."

"Oh, for heaven's sake. Put your arm around me. That'll give you more room."

"Now there's a concept." Grady looked over at Jake. "I'll go first and then you. If we tried to do it at the same time, odds are we'd tip this sofa backward into the teeny, tiny snow village."

"Understood."

Moments after they'd finished the maneuver, Mrs. Gentry wheeled in a tea cart loaded down with mugs of cider and a huge plate of decorated sugar cookies.

Stan got up and Jake started to do the same because that was his training when a lady entered the room.

"Don't try it," Grady warned in an undertone. "You'll throw off the equilibrium and make a mess."

"Right." Jake raised his voice a couple of notches above normal conversational level. "Don't mean to be impolite, Mrs. Gentry, but Grady and I will disrupt everything if we stand."

"Heavens, don't do that." She handed Stan two mugs and the plate of cookies before turning toward the sofa. "One of you big boys could have had my chair."

"Thank you, ma'am," Jake said. "But we're fine right here."

"You look mighty squished up to me, but when you're courtin', that's probably how you like it." She gave Sapphire a mug of cider. "Is that an engagement ring on your finger, Sapphire Ferguson?"

"Yes, Mrs. Gentry, it is. I'd like you to meet my fiancé, Grady Magee."

"Pleased to make your acquaintance, young man." She beamed at Grady. "Well done. Sapphire's a catch."

"Yes, ma'am, she is."

"When's the big day?"

"We're working on that," Sapphire said. "We have tight schedules."

"Tight saddles? Then you need Ben Radcliffe to loosen them up. He's—"

"No, *schedules*."

"Oh, *schedules*. I see that problem a lot with young people these days. I hope you find the time, but at least you've found each other. That's the important part."

When the older woman turned her attention to the other half of the sofa's residents, Jake could guess what was coming. He wondered how Amethyst would handle it. After all, he had his arm around her and he was out caroling with the family. He must look suspiciously like a significant person in Amethyst's life.

Apparently, Amethyst decided to take the initiative. She had such amazing voice control that she could subtly turn up the volume without shouting. "Mrs. Gentry, this is Jake Ramsey. Remember I dated him in high school?

He lives in Jackson Hole now, but he came over for a couple of days so we invited him to go caroling with us for old time's sake."

"That's nice." Mrs. Gentry handed him a mug of cider. "Enjoying yourself, Jake Ramsey?"

"Yes, ma'am."

"Thought so." She gave him a wink before taking the plate of cookies from Stan and offering them to the couch sitters. At last everyone had been served, so she took her cider over to the recliner.

Once she was settled in, she lifted her mug. "To love!" When everyone echoed her toast, she smiled. "Nothing else matters, you know. Now, drink up. I have plenty more where this came from."

The cider turned out to be delicious and sneakily potent. Two mugs of the stuff and Jake could feel the effects, so he wondered if Amethyst, being much lighter, might be getting smashed. That would explain why her conversation had become more animated and she'd allowed her free hand to rest lightly on his thigh. Fine with him.

Jane was the one who finally got them all moving toward the door. Mrs. Gentry insisted they take a Tupperware container of cookies and Jane accepted it with a smile and a loud thank-you. Miraculously they all donned coats, hats and scarfs without dumping the cookies or breaking any of the fragile items crowding the room. But the coat tree would have fallen into the Christmas tree if Jake hadn't grabbed the top at the last minute.

"Yay, Jake!" Amethyst blew him a kiss. "My hero!"

Yeah, she was definitely toasted. That meant they'd hang out at her folks' house longer than he might have planned because he didn't want her driving until the cider had worn off. Food would help a lot, though.

At last they were all standing on the sidewalk and, once again, Jane took charge. "I propose we end this caroling gig and go fix some dinner."

"Good idea." Stan wrapped an arm around her shoulders and headed down the sidewalk toward home. "That cider packed a punch."

Sapphire and Grady followed, arms around each other's waists. Sapphire started giggling. "But it sure beats the heck out of *surstromming*! I'll carol at Mrs. Gentry's any old day."

"Me, too." Stan called back to her. "But next year we're reversing the order and ending with her house."

"Works for me." Amethyst gazed up at Jake. "How 'bout you?"

"I'd go along with that." He'd had his arm over her shoulder the whole time they'd been on the sofa and he saw no reason to hesitate now. He tucked her against his side as they followed Grady and Sapphire.

Amethyst slid her arm around his waist as naturally as if they'd picked up where they'd left off when they'd dated in high school. "Although I might not be able to come home for Christmas next year." She didn't sound very tipsy now.

"I know." He wondered if the cold air had sobered her up. Or it could be the realization that she couldn't blithely make plans with her family if she intended to follow through on her move.

"Because I've kept my overhead low by living here, I've had the luxury of turning down any gigs that would take me away over Christmas. My parents could have avoided having my dad work through the holiday if they hadn't had kids."

"I'm sure neither of them regrets that."

"I'm sure they don't, either. I probably won't regret giving up Christmas with my family if it means I'll get my big break."

"Probably not." But he was glad she was taking the necessary sacrifices into consideration.

"I just happened to think of something. Do you stand to make more money if you stay in Jackson Hole?"

"Quite likely. It's been a vacation playground for the rich and famous for a while, and chances are the area will grow faster and bigger than Sheridan because it's so close to Yellowstone. I considered that a plus when I got the job, but money isn't everything."

Amethyst chuckled. "So I've heard. I hope you know I'm not into this music thing for the money."

"I've never thought that. But I may not be clear on what you do want out of this career."

"To fulfill my potential."

That sounded like something a teacher might have said to her. "And what does that mean, exactly?"

"I've been told I have the voice to be a major recording star, so, obviously, since I'm not a major recording star, I haven't fulfilled my potential."

He didn't know how to respond without risking the fight Chelsea had warned him about. Amethyst must not value the contribution she was making now or she wouldn't say something like that. He thought what she was doing, entertaining locally and teaching kids, had great value, but he hesitated to tell her. She might take it the wrong way, as if he wanted to keep her here for his own selfish purposes.

"So what's the deal with Marla?"

He almost said Marla who? He'd forgotten about her already, which wasn't fair to Marla. He made a mental note that he couldn't let his old flame think he was interested when he clearly wasn't. If and when they communicated again, he'd make sure she understood that he was…what? Unable to focus on anyone but Amethyst? No, he couldn't say that even if it turned out to be true.

"You don't have to tell me. It's none of my business."

"It is while you and I are still involved. Marla and I dated for a while. It didn't go anywhere."

"In case you didn't pick up on it, she's ready to revisit the idea."

"I picked up on it. I didn't want to be rude on Christmas night with everyone standing around listening. I'll handle it later."

She was quiet for a while, but finally she spoke. "I'm a bad person."

"You're absolutely not, so why are you saying it?"

"Because I'm happy that you have no plans to get it on with Marla once I'm out of the picture. But that's completely unfair. We both know that if I achieve what I'm going for in LA, it will be the end of anything between us. If I care about you, and I do, I should *want* you to find someone else!"

Sapphire turned around. "Everything okay back there?"

"Yeah, fine," Jake said. "Just having a deep discussion."

"Okay." Sapphire smiled and hooked her arm around Grady again.

Jake envied the hell out of them. He wanted to be like Grady, who was walking down the street knowing that he had a future with the woman nestled against his hip. Instead Amethyst wanted to discuss his plan to replace her after she'd moved away.

He sucked in a lungful of cold air. "Let's take one thing at a time, shall we? You haven't even left yet. I'm not going to troll for a new girlfriend while you're still in Wyoming. As for Marla, when I saw her tonight I had the fleeting thought I should probably stay in touch in order to hedge my bets."

"Aha! See, I knew—"

"But then the evening continued, and we had a great time with Mrs. Gentry, and you sat on her sofa with your hand on my thigh and—"

"Hang on. I did no such thing!"

"Sorry, but you did."

"I put my hand on your thigh in front of *everybody*?"

"Yes, but it's possible nobody else noticed. I couldn't very well miss it. My thigh is extremely sensitive, especially when you're stroking it."

Her voice rose. "I was *stroking* it?"

Sapphire glanced over her shoulder again. "Just so you know, I'm getting little snippets and my imagination's going wild up here."

"Mine, too," Grady said. "I must've been drunker than I thought if I missed stroking action going on."

"Calm yourselves," Jake said. "It's not what you're thinking."

"Then what is it?" Sapphire asked.

"Nothing," Amethyst said. "Absolutely nothing."

Sapphire laughed. "Yeah, okay. We'll talk later."

"Good idea, sis."

In the silence that followed, Jake hoped she'd forgotten all about his ex-girlfriend.

She cleared her throat. "So. Back to Marla."

No such luck. "What about her?"

This time she kept her voice low. "Look, it's fine and perfectly logical for you to keep her number in case you might want to call her later. Why wouldn't you do that?"

"Because she's not an option, regardless. Taking up with her after being with you would be like dealing with a brush fire in somebody's backyard after battling a two-thousand-acre forest fire in Yellowstone."

"I'm a two-thousand-acre forest fire? That doesn't sound like a good thing."

"In terms of firefighting, it's not." He hugged her close. "But in terms of passionate loving, it's a very good thing."

15

AMETHYST HAD MORE fun at her parents' dinner table that night than she'd had in ages. She'd always enjoyed hanging with her folks, but having Grady and Jake there changed the dynamic in ways she couldn't have imagined. The foster brothers couldn't help teasing each other, which fit right in with her dad's sense of humor.

He'd held his own in a house full of women for years, but tonight he clearly got a charge out of having male allies. She had a rare glimpse of what he must have been like when he'd been a single guy traveling with a band. Yet when he'd had a chance to make that his life, he'd chosen a different path.

She was at that same crossroads, and her parents and her sister and Grady provided a live demonstration of what she would be giving up. Dedication to her art, especially when it involved popular music, required sacrifice. Professor Edenbury had drummed that into her. But sitting at the dinner table surrounded by love, she felt a twinge of doubt that such a sacrifice would make her happy.

Then again, Mrs. Gentry's cider might be making her

more nostalgic than usual. It definitely had been a factor in loosening everybody up. As Amethyst wiped away tears of laughter while Jake and Grady danced around the table singing "Grandma Got Run Over by a Reindeer," she knew she'd remember the moment for the rest of her life. She wanted to be alone with Jake, but when the hour grew late and it was past time to leave, she lingered. Given her plans, this kind of evening might never happen again and she hated to see it end.

When she and Jake finally stood in the entry with their coats on, her mom handed her a bag full of Mrs. Gentry's cookies and gave her a fierce hug. "All I want for you is happiness," she murmured.

"I know, Mom." She hugged her back with equal doses of love and gratitude. "Thank you for inviting Jake tonight. It was special."

Her mother gazed at her with affection shining in her eyes. "It was. I enjoyed seeing him again." She paused, as if about to say something else, but gave a little shake of her head as if deciding not to. "How about having coffee at Rangeland Roasters before you head off to Jackson Hole for your gig?"

"Sounds great." She wouldn't be meeting her mom for coffee every week, either. Change was hard, but progress couldn't be made without it. She hugged her dad and then preceded Jake out the door. "Hey, it's snowing!" she called over her shoulder to her parents.

"Drive carefully!" her dad said.

"Want me to drive you?" Jake followed her down the porch steps. "I can bring you back here to pick up your car on my way out of town in the morning."

That was so Jake, wanting to keep her safe. "Thanks,

but I'd rather drive it home now. It's not too bad, yet. We'll go slow."

"Okay. I'll follow you."

On the way back to her house she navigated the road with extra care because she didn't want Jake to worry. That was ironic, because he would worry himself to death when she left for LA. But of all the hazards in that city, both real and imagined, driving in snow wouldn't be one of them.

She could try pointing that out to Jake and her family but she doubted it would have any effect on their misgivings. Driving in snow was a known quantity that everyone in Wyoming had learned how to handle. LA was full of the unknown. She was scared, too, and unfortunately her nearest and dearest weren't helping.

By the time she pulled into her driveway, the snow had let up a bit. Big flakes drifted lazily down for a snow-globe effect. She'd never minded snow. As a kid she'd spent hours playing in it, and sometimes she and Sapphire still did. Or they used to before Sapphire moved to Cody.

She and Grady were staying another day before heading back, so if this snowfall kept up all night, they might be up for building a snowman. Amethyst wanted to grab such opportunities while she could. Although she missed her sister now, it would be worse once they were more than a thousand miles apart.

Jake's light rap on the window startled her and she jumped.

"Are you okay?" His voice was muted by the closed window, but she could tell from his expression that he was concerned.

She nodded and quickly unfastened her seat belt. Then she grabbed her purse and the bag of cookies.

He opened the door as she started to climb down. Then he lifted her out and into his arms. "You were just sitting there. I thought something was wrong."

"Sorry if I scared you. I got caught up in memories of making snowmen with Sapphire when we were kids."

"You were still building them when we were dating." He reached around her and nudged her door closed. "I remember a really elaborate one you two made over the Thanksgiving weekend of our senior year."

"The pilgrim couple! I'd forgotten all about that. Sapphire was the mastermind behind it. I just did what she told me. It's no wonder she and Grady get along so well. Two peas in a pod."

He drew her closer. "I hear California is chock-full of musicians. Maybe you'll find your matching pea over there."

He might be teasing but she didn't think so. At least she could put his mind to rest on that score. "That's not the goal. I'm going over there to see if I can make it as a recording artist, not look for a soul mate. Besides, that life is hard on relationships. I can't imagine how tough it must be to maintain a connection with someone when you're completely focused on the work."

"Sounds like you've made peace with that."

"I have, Jake." She looked into his eyes. "I may never live like my folks or Sapphire and Grady. That doesn't mean I won't cherish every moment I've spent with you."

"Same here." He searched her expression a moment longer before he visibly pulled himself together. "You know what? We have more of those moments available before I leave. Give me those cookies." Wrapping his other arm around her shoulders, he hurried her toward the porch and up the steps. "First thing in the door, boots off."

"Aw, no wild sex on the floor with our boots on?" She fished out her key and inserted it in the lock.

"Yes to wild sex on the floor. No to doing it with our boots on." Once the door was open he hustled her inside and leaned against the wall to remove them. "It's Christmas night. We should make love under the tree."

"We won't fit unless you plan to lop some branches off the bottom."

"Literal woman, aren't you? *Near* the tree. I want to see the lights make a rainbow on your naked body like they did last night." He put down the cookies, shrugged out of his coat and threw it on the sofa. "But your floor is hard. We're bringing bedding down here this time." He helped her out of her coat, grabbed her hand and started toward the stairs.

She had to hustle to keep up with him. She was gasping by the time they reached the landing. "Hang on a minute. I don't go for five-mile runs like some people."

"Oh, sorry. I was thinking with my dick."

"Just let me catch my breath."

Glancing back at her, he gave a short nod. "Right. I should've done this in the first place." In one smooth motion he hoisted her over his shoulder and carried her the rest of the way with her ass in the air.

"Jake!"

"What?" He set her back on her feet and smiled. He wasn't even breathing hard. "Everyone should experience the fireman's carry at least once in their lives, so there you go."

"You're showing off."

"Yes, ma'am." He walked into the bedroom, pulled off the comforter and thrust it into her arms. Then he piled a blanket on top of the comforter, nearly blocking her view. "If you'll take that, I'll get the pillows and the sheets."

"You've obviously put a lot of thought into this fantasy."

"I had some thinking time while I was following you over here." He began stripping off the holiday sheets. "We only have a few hours left and I want to make them count."

"Does that mean you have other schemes in mind once this is checked off your list?"

"Maybe." He bundled up the sheets and added them to his pile. "How about you?"

"I haven't fully accepted that this will be our last night together in this house. The reality hasn't hit me yet."

He turned toward her. "It doesn't have to be the last night." His tone was casual but there was an underlying tension in his words. "If I rent from you, you're welcome to come back and visit anytime."

"You make it sound as if you'll have my room ready and waiting for me."

"Not just your room." He gave her a wicked grin.

Oh, yeah, she could picture coming back to visit Jake and the hot time they'd have. "I appreciate the invitation, but that's not fair to you."

"Why not?"

"Because, as we've said, you need to be free to date someone else. Maybe I didn't like the idea that you'd immediately hook up with Marla, but I also don't want to think of you living in the house waiting for the day when I..." She stared at him as the realization struck. "Is that the idea, Jake? You'll keep this place ready for my eventual return? Because you think I probably *will* be back?"

"No."

"Because if that's your motivation for renting from me, you can forget about it."

He divested her of the comforter and blanket before drawing her into his arms. "I don't want you to come back. Not permanently, anyway."

"Liar."

"Yeah, well, I do, but that's not what *you* hope for, so I'll be rooting really hard for you to make it big over there." He rubbed the small of her back. "Please believe me, Amethyst. I want whatever you want. I'm not trying to sabotage you."

She knew him now, knew she could trust him not to lie to her. "Okay, I believe you."

His shoulders relaxed. "That's a relief, although I don't want to be misleading, either. I expect you to succeed. God knows you're talented enough, but we both know life isn't fair. So I thought if I kept the house the way it is, then if the unthinkable happens and something goes wrong..."

At first she was touched, but the more she thought about his plan the less she liked it. It wasn't good for either of them. Then she remembered something else Professor Edenbury had said. "I'm supposed to burn the boats."

"What?"

"It's a military strategy but it applies whenever a goal is set. First you land the army on the beach. Then you burn the boats so retreat isn't an option."

"Did Chelsea say that?"

"No, it was my voice teacher and he made an excellent point. Your reason for keeping the house unchanged is very sweet and so like you, but I just realized that I can't let you rent this place."

He frowned. "What if you take out the furniture and turn the studio back into a bedroom like you talked about before? Would that do it?"

"Not if I know you're living here. I'd still have a connection to the house. And you'd still have a connection to me, and you really need to move on. You might hesitate to do that if you're staying in what used to be my house."

He held her gaze for several seconds. Then he sighed. "Let's forget it."

"I'm sorry. I know you like this place but—"

"I can find something else. You're right. I didn't want you to burn the boats. You built that studio with loving care and I hated to think of you ripping it apart. I see now that you have to give up the house entirely."

And Jake, too. She had a feeling that unless she made a clean break with him he'd imagine they could keep this thing going somehow. He hadn't dated anyone else since August, which should have told her this was more than a fling for him. She hadn't dated anyone, either. Clearly they weren't suited for casual sex.

"Hey." He hugged her closer. "You don't have to burn any boats tonight. Let's carry this stuff downstairs and burn up the sheets instead."

She allowed the passion in his eyes to make her forget everything but this moment. When he looked at her like that, nothing else mattered. "Great idea."

After they carried the bedding downstairs, Jake took over the arrangement and she stood back to watch.

"I wouldn't be upset if you ditched your clothes while I'm doing this," he said. "You'd save us time."

Laughing, she undressed, but she kept an eye on the proceedings as he made up the bed quickly and efficiently. "You've done this before." Her stupid heart felt a pang of jealousy at the idea he'd lovingly made up a similar bed for another woman.

"When I was a kid."

Oh. Not for another woman, after all. Her chest tightened. He'd probably smuggled bedding into whatever secret place he'd used to get away from his father every night. He might still associate a bed on the floor with an escape from reality.

They could both use an escape tonight. As he shook out the top sheet, she finished taking off everything except her bra and matching panties. They were Christmas red, with holly embroidered on them—a sprig over each nipple and one strategically placed on the front of the panties. He'd asked her to undress herself, but these last items were his to remove.

"Done." He tossed back the top sheet before glancing at her. "Hel-lo, Christmas fantasy." He unsnapped the cuffs of his Western shirt as he came toward her. "Humor me and say you bought that combo strictly for my benefit."

"I did."

"Really?" He took off his shirt and dropped it to the floor before reaching for her. "When?"

"Yesterday morning, before I came out to the ranch." She nestled against him and ran her palms up his sculpted chest. "I saved them for tonight. They're not exactly a Christmas present but—"

"Oh, yeah, they are." Heat flared in his eyes as he stepped away from her and held out his hand. "Come on, fantasy lady. Time to unwrap my present."

16

JAKE WAS DOING his damnedest to keep from saying or doing anything that would set off an explosion, but it wasn't easy. That little speech about burning the boats sounded idealistic and noble, but it didn't fit this situation, at least not in his opinion. Besides, had this professor who'd spouted off on the subject burned any boats or did he or she simply stay in the safety of the classroom and pass out that advice to impressionable students?

But it wasn't Jake's place to question the strategy or anything else, for that matter. In fact, his impromptu invitation to have her come back and visit had almost ruined everything. He'd managed to contain the damage, but now she didn't want him to rent the house, which sucked.

For the next few hours he'd better concentrate on the one thing they definitely agreed on. He doubted he'd change her mind with great sex, but he'd have a hell of a good time trying.

She stretched out on the bed he'd created, tucked a pillow under her head and the effect was outstanding. Christmas lights splashed color over her delicious-looking skin and his mouth watered.

The house had been chilly last night when she'd been naked beside the tree, but it was warmer now. He'd be willing to bet she'd turned up the heat before leaving for her parents' house today. He appreciated the advance planning because he intended to use his tongue on every inch of her.

That program would go better in a warm room. She'd bought her outfit for him, too, and he intended to pay special attention to the places currently being covered by red satin decorated with holly. Her erect nipples pushed at the holly decoration, giving it a 3-D effect. Nice.

He stripped off his jeans and briefs and laid the jeans within reach because of the condoms tucked in the pockets.

"You look good in Christmas lights," she murmured. Her attention was fixed on his package and her tongue swept over her plump lips. She crooked a finger at him. "Come down here."

His balls tightened. He'd spent enough naked time with her that he recognized that husky tone. He had a game plan but she might have one, too. Tonight he would deny her nothing.

He dropped slowly to his knees beside her. "What can I do for you?"

Her blue eyes were smoky with desire as she wrapped her warm fingers around his cock. "I want this."

He nearly came. "And just how do you want it?"

"I want to taste you."

Although having him above her for this particular pleasure was new, he didn't have to be a genius to figure it out. Responding to her gentle tug, he straddled her. "Don't make me come."

Her soft laughter tickled the sensitive tip, already moist from wanting her. "Why not?"

"I'll be out of commission for a while."

"Not for long. I know you. Now, lean forward. I want to play."

He flattened his palms on either side of the pillow and surrendered to her mouth. Sweet heaven, the woman knew how to play. His fingers curled into the sheet as her tongue danced and her cheeks hollowed. Then, because she was in the perfect position for it, she cupped his balls and began a slow massage.

He groaned, hoping that would relieve the pressure building as he fought the urge to come. But the vibration in his chest only increased the erotic sensations swirling around him. He gasped as she raked her teeth along the underside of his cock.

He'd probably known from the moment he let her take the lead that he was done for. She loved giving him an orgasm as much as he loved giving her one. As his control slipped away, he abandoned himself to extreme pleasure. She seemed to know exactly how to touch him, when to squeeze, how to lick, where to bite.

At the moment when he completely let go, it was with the knowledge that she was the best thing to ever come into his life. He might lose her. In fact, he probably would. But as he whirled in the grip of a shattering climax, he knew the eventual pain was worth this. Oh, yeah, *this*.

Eventually the roaring in his ears subsided and his muscles responded to his commands. He managed to flop down on his back beside her on the makeshift bed, but his breathing was still ragged. "That wasn't how I intended this adventure to go."

"That's how I intended it to go."

"Oh, really?" He turned his head to find her gazing at him. "Since when?"

"Since you threw me over your shoulder like some modern-day caveman. I felt the need to create a balance of power."

"But you've always had the power."

"I don't *think* so. You're the one who broke up with me in high school, remember?"

"Self-preservation. Even then I knew that you had the power and it freaked me out."

"But not anymore?"

"Oh, no, it still freaks me out, but for a blow job like that I'll deal with it." He wanted to lighten the mood and he'd succeeded.

She laughed and rolled to face him. "When this started between us in August, I—"

"It started long before that." He mirrored her position so he could look into her eyes.

"Okay, when we were juniors, planning for the junior-senior prom."

"Bingo. I volunteered to help and there you were. I was toast."

"I never got that impression." She reached over and traced the curve of his eyebrows. "I thought you were mildly interested."

"I was a heat-seeking missile, which scared the crap out of me because I was a virgin and terrified of getting a girl pregnant."

"I was a virgin, too."

"I never guessed. I believed I'd fallen for the sexiest, most experienced girl in the junior class. I thought about you all summer."

"I thought about you, too."

"You're kidding."

"No, Jake, I'm not. I kept hoping that I'd run into you that summer, but you were out at the ranch and I was in town. It never happened."

"My bad luck."

"Or not. By the time school started I was determined to ask you out. If I hadn't been so persistent I'm not sure we would have dated."

He sighed. "Forgive me for being an idiot." He skimmed her hip with a light touch. "You wanted me and I loused it up."

"No you didn't." She cupped his face in both hands. "If you hadn't broken up with me, you would have been my first, and we would have attached so much significance to the experience at that age. Instead my first was someone I didn't love and I never went out with him again."

"What's good about that story? That first time is supposed to be special."

"Was yours?"

"No, but that was my own fault. There was a party and I was slightly drunk. Never should have happened but she was persistent and I was stupid. We never went out again, either."

"See? Let's say you hadn't broken up with me and we'd done the deed senior year."

"It would have been special." And, damn it, he wished he could rewrite history.

"I'm sure it would have been, and we could be married by now. We might have kids. Maybe you wouldn't be a firefighter and I definitely wouldn't be moving to LA. It all worked out for the best."

Obviously he was supposed to agree with her. He swallowed his initial response, something along the lines of *bullshit*, and confirmed the part that he did happen to agree with. "Yeah, we were too young for that kind of intense relationship. At least I was. I had a lot to learn." Although he'd known couples that helped each other grow up. One of his buddies at the station had married his childhood sweetheart and after twenty years they were closer than ever.

"I had plenty to learn, too." She smiled at him. "I still do."

"Not me. I've achieved total perfection."

Her eyebrows arched. "Is that so?"

"Ask anybody." He pulled her close. "I know all, see all. I can even read minds. Right now you're thinking *a little less talk and a little more action*. Am I right?"

"No, you're not, smarty-pants. I like talking to you."

"Of course you do, because I'm a brilliant conversationalist." He rolled her to her back, which was fun to do when they were both laughing. "But let's be honest, that's not the most spectacular thing I can do with my mouth. And I know you, Amethyst Ferguson. You want some of that."

Her blue eyes sparkled with a mixture of laughter and lust. "Yes I do, you conceited man. Lay your amazing perfection on me immediately."

"You've got it." Capturing her wrists, he stretched them above her head and manacled them with one hand while he looked into her eyes and stroked her warm skin. "I can't wait to play with my Christmas present."

Her breathing changed. "I hope you like it."

"I know I will." Lowering his head, he nibbled on her mouth while he stroked the sleek satin covering her breasts. "When you put this on this morning, did you think of me touching you here?"

"Yes." She arched upward so she could thrust her breast into his palm. "And now I want it off."

"Are you going to tell me how to unwrap my present?"

"I'm only making suggestions as the owner of the bra. There's a front catch, so if you…" She sucked in a breath as he flipped it open and pushed the fabric away so he could massage at will. "Mmm, like that."

"Glad you approve."

"Turn me loose and I can take it all the way off."

"Okay." He couldn't help smiling. "Still giving directions, I see." He loosened his hold on her wrists and helped her out of it.

"Once it's unfastened it serves no purpose."

"I wouldn't say that." He grabbed the bra before she could toss it aside. "I've always believed in reusing Christmas wrapping."

"For what?"

"A game." He captured her wrists again and drew them over her head. Then he wound the bra several times around her wrists.

"Jake Ramsey, are you getting kinky on me?" Her breathy question sounded as if she sincerely hoped so.

"A little bit. Hold still while I fasten the hooks. How does that feel?"

"Like I'm no longer in charge of this operation."

He cupped her cheek while he feathered a kiss over her mouth. "Yeah, you are. Do you want it undone?"

"No." Her voice vibrated with excitement.

"See, I knew that because I can read your mind." He ran his tongue over her lower lip as he pulled the flimsy material of her panties aside so he could explore.

"Then why ask me?"

"It turns me on to hear you say you like it."

"I've never let anybody do this before."

"But you let me." He slid his fingers into her wet channel.

"Because you're… Jake." She gasped out his name as he circled her clit with his thumb.

He left the velvet softness of her mouth and kissed his way to her full breast. "Perfection." Drawing her nipple into his mouth, he rolled it over his tongue while he pumped his fingers in a slow rhythm.

"Perfection…perfect—oh…ohhh." Lifting her hips, she silently asked for more.

He delved deeper and found her G-spot as he continued to suck on her tight nipple. Her soft whimper became a wail, then a series of panting breaths and finally a lusty cry that made him shiver with happiness. Her orgasm undulated across his fingers and he savored the pleasure of knowing he'd made her come.

She was still shuddering in reaction when he moved down and wedged his shoulders under her hips. He sacrificed one precious moment to admire the play of Christmas lights over her quivering body. Then he lifted her to his waiting mouth, nudged her panties aside and coaxed her to come again. Gasping and moaning his name, she writhed against the sheets.

His bed was coming undone but so was she, and that was all that mattered. He'd vowed to drive her crazy tonight and, judging from her wild cries, he was succeeding. As she lay panting beneath him, he made a slow journey back up her moist, hot body, kissing and licking a pathway to her breasts, her throat and, finally, her lips. The flavor of her climax was still on his tongue as he thrust it deep.

She kissed him back with such heat that he knew she was ready for more. Sliding his hands up her arms, he unbound her wrists. She responded by gripping his head, her fingertips pressing against his scalp as she held him steady so that she could ravish his mouth.

"Take me." Her urgent plea was followed by equally urgent kisses.

The pressure in his cock was almost past enduring. He fumbled blindly for his jeans and by some miracle snagged his finger in a pocket. The condom seemed to leap into his hand. Breaking away from her hungry kiss, he pushed back onto his knees. No condom in the history of birth control had been rolled on this quickly.

She reached for his hips. "Now, Jake. I want you inside me."

"I want that, too." His words were choked with the intensity of his need for her. "More than you could ever know." Poised between her welcoming thighs, he allowed the tip of his cock to slip easily into her wet channel. Then he leaned down and locked his gaze with hers. "Hang on. This might be intense." Before she could respond, he pushed his hips forward and did exactly what she'd asked. He took her.

The phrase implied vigorous action, so he gave her that. Full throttle, no holds barred. Her breasts trembled with the force of his cock driving deep.

But he wasn't a conquering hero. He was her lover, at least for this brief space of time. So he paused, gasping. "Talk to me. Are you okay?"

She gulped for air. "Never better. Go for it."

So he did, but then as he felt his orgasm approaching and knew hers was very close, too, he felt the need to slow things down. Words welled up inside him, words he'd never allowed himself to say. Yet if he didn't say them now, he might never have the chance.

Vaguely he understood that saying those words would change everything. But she'd told him to go for it, and that could be interpreted more than one way. Orgasms were wonderful, but without the words he longed to say, what did they mean?

So instead of rocketing forward to a blazing mutual climax, he eased back on the throttle. Sure, his cock protested, but he was in charge, not the bad boy who only cared about instant gratification. A great deal was at stake, and leaving things unsaid was not a good strategy.

Amethyst, being a very smart woman, noticed the change in mood immediately. She glanced up at him. "Is something wrong?"

"No, but I need to tell you something." He maintained a steady rhythm, but it was nothing like the balls-to-the-wall pace he'd kept up before.

"Can't it wait?"

"I don't think so."

She must have had a hint of what was coming, because her blue eyes became a little misty. "I have a feeling this is something best left unsaid."

"You're probably right." He rocked forward, settling into her warmth before instinct made him ease back to create the same friction all over again. Sometimes he wondered why this connection between a man and a woman had to be so complicated. These were the basics. The rest was just details.

"Then don't say it." She bracketed his hips and held on tight. "Just concentrate on the pleasure we give each other." She rose to meet his thrust. "Isn't that enough?"

"Not anymore. You don't want to hear it, but I have to say it. Amethyst, I love you."

Her gaze filled with longing. "Oh, Jake."

"I can't help it. Every minute, every second, with you feels so right. I used to think we didn't belong together, but not anymore."

She reached up to cradle his face in both hands. "We don't belong together," she murmured.

"Why? Because you don't love me?"

"I didn't say that."

"You can't say it because it's not true." He kept up his lazy rhythm, loving her, wanting her to feel and acknowledge the unbelievable connection between them. "Admit it. You're in love with me."

"What if I am?" Her words were tinged with regret. "That doesn't change anything."

He paused to gaze down at her. "It doesn't?"

"No." Her voice was husky with emotion. "I was in love with you in high school. I'm in love with you now. That won't affect my decision to leave."

He knew she meant what she was saying. She thought herself capable of sacrificing love for her music career. She imagined herself burning those boats. Not tonight, but soon.

But as she lay warm and succulent in his arms, he had a hard time believing it. She loved everything about her life in Sheridan. She loved him. The woman he'd come to know wouldn't throw everything away because some college professor had told her she should.

17

Amethyst had never been loved so well or so thoroughly, and she knew why. Jake was right. They did belong together, except for one small detail. She'd decided to walk a different path.

When he left their cozy bed to dispose of the condom in the kitchen, she lay gazing up at the lights on the tree. Then it hit her. The problem was Christmas. The holiday brought out emotions, both good and bad, that lay buried the rest of the year. People expected so much of Christmas—marriage proposals, meaningful gifts, declarations of love.

She'd thought meeting Jake in the hardware store was a happy coincidence. Why wouldn't she be thrilled at the prospect of enjoying some hot sex with him during a holiday filled with joy? The timing had seemed perfect, especially after they'd worked out the logistics.

Instead, they'd created the perfect storm. Without Jake's arrival, she wouldn't have met Chelsea or learned about Matt Forrest, a guy who'd spent three years pounding on doors in Hollywood. Meanwhile she'd spent the same amount of time gallivanting around Wyoming hoping to be discovered.

Matt's story had showed her the risk she'd been unwilling to take. Problem was, in the midst of getting clarity on that issue, she'd fallen in love with the man she had to leave behind.

Last summer's encounter had been about sex. Really good sex, too. The kind that made her reluctant to get naked with anyone else while that vivid memory still simmered in her mind and body. But it hadn't been love. That development could be blamed entirely on Christmas.

She'd started to fall when she'd discovered him checking out smoke alarms. Until that moment she hadn't thought much about his occupation or his dedication to it. Then she'd watched him coming in backward in that broken-down sleigh and had eventually realized that he'd invited her for a sleigh ride without being in possession of one.

With each change of scene, the facets of his personality had gleamed in a way she might not have noticed without the Christmas festivities. She'd had a chance to observe him interacting with his family and hers, and she'd admired how easily he fit into either situation. She'd watched him handle a deaf old woman's request with humor, grace and compassion.

She'd learned more about him in the past two days than she had in weeks of dating him in high school. And she'd revealed more about herself. Her family knew that her sexy persona was an act, but she'd never discussed that with anyone else. Dropping that mask had seemed like a natural thing to do with Jake. After all, she'd been falling in love.

The subject of her musings, gloriously naked, walked back into the living room. Only the Christmas tree lights were on, which gave him a mysterious, almost other-worldly appearance as he made a slight detour and picked up something from an end table. Then she recognized what it was and smiled.

"I thought it was time for some of Mrs. Gentry's cookies."

"Excellent thought." She sat up.

"I didn't want to rummage through your refrigerator without asking, but do you have any milk?"

"I have milk and I also have eggnog. Take your pick."

"I'd love some eggnog."

"Me, too." She started to get up.

"Nope." He laid a hand on her bare shoulder. "You stay there and relax. I'll take care of it."

"Glasses are in the top cupboard next to the stove."

"Thanks." He walked back into the kitchen and she admired the view. She'd been too blissed out on great sex to think of it the first time he'd left the room. Wide shoulders, narrow hips, tight buns, muscled thighs and calves—she couldn't imagine a man who would appeal to her physically as much as Jake did.

Even better, he'd developed that body so he could be a better firefighter. Knowing that he'd probably carried people and animals to safety the way he'd hauled her up those stairs made him quite a hero. He deserved a woman who would be there for him, who would want to have children, assuming he did. She hadn't ever asked him and wouldn't. Not a good subject for them.

He returned with the eggnog and a couple of glasses. "I didn't know you liked eggnog."

"Love it. I'm always sad when Christmas is over and it disappears from the shelves."

"I know!" He handed her the glasses and sat on the blanket, facing her. "Why couldn't it be available all the time?" He gave the carton a vigorous shake. "It's not like they couldn't keep making it."

"True." She held out the glasses while he poured. "It could be marketing. If eggnog's available all year, then it wouldn't be special. Think about how wild we were for each other last night. We're much calmer tonight. Give us another week and we'd be watching TV instead of having sex."

"Wrong." He clinked his glass against hers. "To love."

"You and Mrs. Gentry. Both incurable romantics." She sipped her eggnog.

"Whereas you're a flinty-eyed realist." He dug in the bag and handed her a cookie.

"I'm not sure about the flinty-eyed part, but I think I'm pretty realistic." She bit into the cookie, which was shaped like a Christmas tree and covered with green frosting and little candies to simulate ornaments. "She put a lot of work into these."

"She did. When I move back here I plan to go see her."

"And check out her house for fire hazards?"

"That, too. She had a couple of cords that looked compromised and I wonder what kind of wiring she has in that house. It's been there awhile. But mostly I just want to pay her a visit, find out if she needs any errands run, things like that."

She melted. If she hadn't been totally in love with him, that little speech would have done the trick. "What a fabulous idea. I'm sure she'd love having you visit."

"And I'd love doing it." He finished off his cookie and glanced at her. "You're not eating your snack."

"I was imagining you making friends with Mrs. Gentry. If I weren't leaving, I'd go with you."

His gaze sharpened. "You would?"

"Sure. She was always nice to Sapphire and me. Once I moved out of the neighborhood I didn't make the effort to see her very often. Now I wish I had."

"Having you come along would be great."

"Obviously it's not possible, but if I could clone myself, I'd hang around and watch her reaction. She'll get such a kick out of you, Jake."

"I already get a kick out of her."

"That's why you'll be so good for the community. You're focused on helping others and we need people like that."

"Hmm."

"What?"

"Nothing. I just noticed that you…never mind." He took a deep breath. "Do you want the rest of that cookie?"

"You can have it." She handed it to him. "The eggnog filled me up. They're big cookies. I was thinking of offering them to my students. I scheduled a couple of lessons for the twenty-seventh because they'll be bored with vacation by then, anyway. But one of those and they'd be on a sugar high. I'll have to come up with something else because I like giving them a little treat after the lesson."

"You won't have to worry about it much longer, though."

"That's true." She sighed. "I'm not sure what to do about those kids. Nobody else in town is offering private voice lessons and I hate to see them quit. You should hear those cuties sing, Jake. They're amazing!"

"Wish I could."

"They're all coming along so well, too, but there's no one to take over after I leave. Well, there's one person but he's not good with the little ones. He yells. They'd be better off with no one than him. The elementary school music teacher has her own children and really doesn't have the time."

Jake drained the last of his eggnog and set the glass aside. "But that's really not your concern. You can't let those kids keep you from going to LA."

"I won't. I'm just worried about them."

He gazed at her for quite a while. "I can see that."

"Something's bothering you."

"Let me ask you a question. After you graduated with your music degree, after you'd heard that advice about burning the boats, why didn't you pack up and move to LA?"

Her chest tightened. "Because I wasn't ready."

"Then why didn't you go last summer?"

"You know why." She began to shake. "I'd figured out how to live on what I was able to make and every time I performed somewhere, there was a chance someone would be in the audience who could make it happen for me."

"But you've decided to abandon that strategy. You're ready to burn the boats. Why now?"

"Because I've been procrastinating! I realized that after talking to Chelsea. Professor Edenbury was right. I have to risk everything and just go!"

"Why?"

"Haven't you been listening? I have the talent and I'm wasting it!"

"I don't see it that way." He reached for her.

She wiggled away. "Don't. Don't try to hold me and soothe me like you would an agitated horse. I'm getting a picture here and it's not a pretty one. I thought you were on my side, but you're not, are you?"

"I am! I want the best for you, but is your plan to charge off to LA what's best? You love it here. You have family, friends, students and a recording studio. What's wrong with building a career out of that?"

"What's wrong? I have the ability to be so much more."

"Yes, you do. But will achieving that give you more satisfaction, more happiness? After watching and listening for two days, I doubt it. What if you forget about what some professor put in your head and think about what *you* want? If it's fame and all that goes with it, then fine. But if you really wanted that, it's likely you would have been on the bus for LA the minute you graduated."

"Not necessarily!" Rage coursed through her. "How dare you say such a thing? You don't know a damn thing about this, Jake. So butt out, okay?" She scrambled to her feet and hurried over to the sofa to grab her coat. It was the fastest way she could think of to hide. She hadn't felt naked before, but she sure as hell did now.

He sighed and hung his head. "Damn me for a fool. I kept telling myself not to say anything, to enjoy the sex and keep my mouth shut." When he looked up at her, his eyes were filled with misery. "But I love you, and I think somebody should tell you the truth. You're not wasted here. You're in your element. You can perform, and teach, and hang out with your family. What could be better?"

She hugged her coat around her. "You know the worst part of this? I can't even accuse you of saying this for your benefit because that's not who you are. You're saying this for *my* benefit. You're trying to clip my wings for my own good."

"I'm not trying to clip your wings, damn it!" Getting to his feet, he began pulling on his clothes. "There are different ways to soar, Amethyst. You don't have to top the charts to have liftoff, to affect people's lives in positive ways. You're doing it now and you love every minute of it."

"You think I can't make it."

"Oh, no, I think you can." He paused to gaze at her. "And that would be the real tragedy."

She swallowed. "Let yourself out. I'm going up to my studio."

"Amethyst…"

"It's over, Jake. It would have been eventually, so maybe this is better. Goodbye." She ran up the stairs and adrenaline gave her the necessary boost to make it to the top without stopping for breath. The memory of Jake throwing her over his shoulder hurt like hell, but she'd get past it. Besides, she wouldn't be in this house much longer anyway.

JAKE STARED AFTER her and debated going up there. Then he heard a lock click and knew he'd have to break down her studio door, and that wouldn't help matters. He'd caused the explosion he'd been trying so hard to avoid, but her comments about her students had been the final straw.

As he'd listened to her rave about those kids, he'd realized that if everybody danced around the issue of her leaving, she was liable to do it. She'd hurt herself, her family and those children she was mentoring. She'd also hurt him, but he'd been willing to take the blows. He wasn't willing to stand silently by and let her do this to herself and others. So he'd said what was in his heart.

Chelsea had predicted she wouldn't like it and she definitely hadn't. She'd ordered him out of her house and locked herself in her studio so there was no recourse. She'd soundproofed the walls, but the vibration of a heavy bass made the whole house shiver.

After he finished dressing, he folded all the bedding and laid it on the sofa. Then he rinsed the glasses in the kitchen sink and closed up the bag of cookies. At least he had a place to go. In the old days he would have had to break into a vacant house to find a safe place to sleep. But a key to one of the ranch's log cabins lay in his pocket.

So did several condoms. He grimaced. Wouldn't be using those anytime soon. Before he left he turned off the Christmas tree lights. Even though they were LEDs, he didn't like the idea of leaving them on when nobody was downstairs.

Although he couldn't lock the dead bolt on his way out, he could at least engage the one on the knob. He was out the door before he fully realized how hard it was snowing. He had to fight his way to the truck and wrench the door open. His windshield wipers struggled with the snow piled on them, but they finally cleared a small space that would allow him to drive away from there.

The trip back to the ranch took forever, which gave him way too much time to think. He kept his cell phone on the seat in case he got stuck and had to call someone.

The plows hadn't come out yet and likely wouldn't until morning. Sensible people wouldn't be out on the road at this hour on Christmas night, or rather, the morning of the twenty-sixth.

Christmas was officially over and he'd ended his and Amethyst's holiday with a bang. But when he considered what he'd said to her, he didn't regret a word of it. He deeply regretted that those words had driven a wedge between them, but he'd heard somewhere that it was a tradition to kill the messenger. Come to think of it, he did feel sort of dead inside.

But at the very least, he might have given her something to think about. She was furious now, but when her anger faded, she might remember some of the things he'd said. She might even wonder if any of those ideas held water.

Or maybe that was too much to hope for. He'd have to accept the fact that he could have ruined everything between them and destroyed any happy memories she had of their time together, all for nothing. She could go to LA, after all, cursing his name the whole way.

If she did make the move, he wouldn't hear from her, but he had ways to find out what had happened. He could go through Grady because Sapphire would be dialed in to Amethyst's progress. He wondered if someday he'd turn on the TV and see her, or he'd be listening to the radio and one of her songs would come on.

If so, he prayed she'd be happy with the choices she'd made. He couldn't see how she would be, but she might prove him wrong. She might never forgive him for what he'd said tonight. He'd live with that, just as he'd live with the knowledge that he'd never stop loving her.

18

JAKE WAS UP early the next morning after getting very little sleep in a narrow bunk bed. As a teenager he hadn't minded them. They'd been a hell of a lot better than the makeshift beds he'd created in his hidey-holes. But he'd grown considerably larger since then and he didn't fit anymore.

The bunk hadn't been the main problem but it gave him something to blame for his lack of sleep besides worry over Amethyst. She'd been really upset. Although he was glad he'd said his piece, he hated to think of her in pain, especially when he couldn't do anything about it.

Peering out the cabin window, he saw that the snow had stopped. He had just enough light to do some shoveling before getting cleaned up for breakfast, and shoveling was great for clearing the mind. He used to do a lot of it when he'd lived here—either snow or manure. There had always been plenty of both.

In winter each cabin had been supplied with a snow shovel and apparently the tradition had continued because he found one leaning in the corner. After bundling up, he grabbed the shovel and headed out. Nothing marred the blanket of snow, so he must be the first person out this morning.

Pushing his way through knee-deep drifts, he trudged up to the ranch house and started there. A path from the house to the barn was the first priority. By the time he finished he could smell wood smoke, which meant Rosie had lit a fire and Herb would be coming down to the barn soon. Jake felt good about making that an easier trip for him.

Next he returned to his cabin and cleared the way to the bathhouse. He added a side path for Finn and Chelsea. The lack of footprints on their snow-covered stoop indicated they hadn't ventured out yet.

When the cabins had been built, a communal bathhouse had been the cheapest solution. Braving the cold walk on winter mornings had become a source of pride for the foster brothers and now for the teenagers enrolled at Thunder Mountain Academy. Chelsea hadn't been part of either tradition and yet she seemed fine with it.

The exercise had warmed Jake up enough that his trip to the bathhouse to shower and shave wasn't bad at all. He made it up to the house in time to help Rosie cook breakfast.

His foster mom looked a little surprised to see him but then she handed him a carton of eggs, a bowl and a whisk. "I love having company when I cook." She gave him a bright smile.

He set to work cracking the eggs into a bowl. "I know I told you I wouldn't be around for breakfast."

"Things change." Rosie started the bacon.

"If Amethyst moves to LA, I doubt she'll be keeping me informed about how it's going, but if you hear anything, would you let me know?"

"Of course." She glanced his way. "Maybe you'd better add another dozen eggs to that bowl. I just remembered that Cade and Lexi are coming for breakfast."

Jake went to the refrigerator and took out another carton. "Has Lexi finally moved in with Cade?"

"Yes." Rosie sounded very happy about that. "She promised me they wouldn't eat all their meals with us, but I don't care if they do. It's fun having them."

"Yeah, but from what I heard, she wants Cade to be more domestic, take on his share of the cooking and such." He added more eggs to the bowl. "I saw the cabin Damon and Phil built for him. Great kitchen."

"I know, and they'll have some of their meals there, I'm sure. Maybe they'll even invite Herb and me up for dinner, which would be fun. But I'm used to feeding a crowd, so it feels normal to have a full table."

"Then I'll be sure and invite myself over once I move back."

Rosie spun away from the stove. "You're moving back?"

"I didn't tell you?"

"No, you did not!"

The excitement in her eyes made him smile. "Nothing's for sure, so don't get too excited, but I plan to if I can get on with the fire department. I'm going over there on my way out of town to see what's up."

Rosie put down her spatula and came over to hug him. "That's wonderful news, Jake."

He hugged her back. "Like I said, don't get your hopes up yet. They may not have an opening. But this time I have years of experience to offer, so that should help my cause."

"I have a good feeling about this." She stepped back to gaze at him. "I've missed you."

The love in her eyes brought a lump to his throat. "I've missed you, too, Mom."

"Hey, there, Jake!" Herb walked into the kitchen. "I didn't think you'd be joining us this morning."

"He's moving back to Sheridan!" Rosie turned to her husband. "Isn't that great?"

"You bet!" He came over to give Jake a hug, too. "Does this have anything to do with—"

"No, it doesn't," Rosie said. "This is all about Jake missing us and wanting to come home." The note of finality in her voice was a clear signal that the subject of Amethyst was closed.

The knot of tension in Jake's chest loosened. He might never have Amethyst in his life, but he'd have his foster parents and his foster brothers. That made him one lucky guy.

RANGELAND ROASTERS HAD windows all along the street side of the shop, so Amethyst could see her mother sitting at one of the tables, waiting for her. Her mom smiled and waved. Amethyst's eyes filled with unexpected tears and she dug in her purse for a tissue.

She'd been doing a lot of crying lately and over silly things, like the way her little five-year-old student mispronounced a word in a song and ended up in a fit of giggles. Yesterday she'd been fixing breakfast and sunlight had come through the kitchen window and caught the crystal she'd hung there a couple of years ago. That dancing rainbow had made her cry, too.

Now she was all choked up because her mother had smiled and waved through the coffee shop window.

She'd like to blame her emotional state on Jake, but after crying her eyes out the night he'd left, she hadn't shed another tear on his behalf. Then again, maybe it was his fault.

Just like the angel in *It's a Wonderful Life*, Jake had pointed out all the ways she was connected to this town she called home. She would be missed when she moved to LA and that was a bigger deal for her than she'd acknowledged when she'd made her decision. It wasn't a two-way street, either. She'd miss everything and everybody, especially her sweet mother. And that brought on another bout of tears.

Her mom left her purse to hold the table and stood so they could walk up and order. But then she took a closer look at her daughter and sat again. She motioned Amethyst to do the same. "What's wrong?"

"Nothing. Everything." She dabbed at her eyes.

"Is it Jake?"

"Not exactly." She sighed. "I thought I knew what to do. If I want to make it as a singer, I need to go to LA, right?"

"Probably. If you want to be a really big success, that's quite likely the way to go."

"I'm scared."

"Oh, honey." Her mother reached over and squeezed her hand. "You'll be fine. You have a good head on your shoulders. I shouldn't have said that about the drug dealers living next door. I'm sure that won't happen."

"I'm not scared about what I'll find there. Well, maybe a little, but that's not what's bothering me." She swallowed. "I'm not even scared of failing, although I understand that's a very real possibility. Mostly I'm scared of losing what I have here."

"You can't really lose that. If it doesn't work out, you can always come home."

Amethyst shook her head. "But, see, that's the problem. If I go, I have to do it with all my heart. I can't be thinking about running home at the first sign of trouble. I have to be totally committed to overcoming every obstacle, the way Finn was when he moved to Seattle and Matt was when he went to Hollywood. I have to want it so much that nothing else matters."

Her mother took a deep breath. "You're right."

"So the way I figure it, I have to know in my gut that I'm willing to make the necessary sacrifices and right now I'm not sure if I'm willing to do that."

"Nobody said you had to leave tomorrow. If you need more time to think about it, then I say take what you need."

She nodded. "That's good advice. And before you drive yourself crazy wondering whether to ask about Jake or not, let me put your mind at rest. I won't be seeing him when I go to Jackson Hole. We called it quits."

"I see."

"I know you liked him."

"That has no bearing on the matter."

"It has all kinds of bearing, Mom. I wouldn't want to get serious about someone you hated."

"I doubt that you would, but thanks."

Amethyst sighed with relief. She never remembered loving her mother more than now. "Since we've made it through all that, let's get some coffee. And a doughnut. I ate all Mrs. Gentry's cookies and I crave something loaded with sugar, something that's really bad for me."

The mood lightened considerably after that and she was able to describe the antics of her voice students without bursting into tears. They talked about the art project her mother planned to assign her high school students when classes resumed in January.

As they hugged goodbye outside the coffee shop, her mother glanced at her. "You said you wouldn't be seeing Jake when you go to Jackson Hole, but couldn't he come to your performance if he wanted to?"

"He won't. He knows I wouldn't like that."

Of course now that her mom had planted the idea, she kept thinking about it during the time leading up to her departure for Jackson Hole. The prospect of Jake showing up at her gig didn't horrify her. She wouldn't ask him up to her room again, but seeing him wouldn't be the worst thing in the world. She'd missed him.

On the day she had to leave, she put her suitcase in the car and turned back to look at the Victorian. How would it feel to leave this house for the last time? She'd have to turn over her key to whoever rented her half of it and that would be the end of making breakfast in the kitchen, working in her studio, enjoying the front porch in the summer.

Her stomach hurt at the thought of giving up this house. A few months ago she'd even considered approaching the landlady about selling it to her. She probably had enough savings for a down payment. Except that was the money earmarked for her first few months in LA.

She climbed into the SUV and backed out of the driveway. One thing she knew for sure—if she went to LA she'd take her crystal. But she might not have a spot where it would work. Her kitchen was on the east side and the double window was perfect. No telling what she'd find in LA.

She had to drive down Main Street to get to the highway and she pictured the SUV loaded with all her stuff instead of just one small suitcase. She'd really be leaving. No more coffee dates with her mom and no more shopping in the stores she knew so well. No more recognizing people she knew and stopping to chat.

Usually she played music when she drove, but on this trip she preferred silence. She needed to think. The closer she came to Jackson Hole, the more she wanted to talk with Jake again, but she didn't have time before the show. If he came to the performance, that would be great. She had something important to tell him.

LA was a dream she'd nurtured ever since Professor Edenbury had told her that she had the necessary talent to be a star. Everybody wanted to be a star, right? She'd imagined it from the time she'd been a little kid with a karaoke machine.

Professor Edenbury had given her dream the stamp of approval but, come to think of it, what had he ever done that was brave or risky? He had a great voice but he'd never tested himself on Broadway. He'd never moved to LA to explore the possibilities there. Near as she knew, he'd never recorded a single song.

Instead he'd expected Amethyst to do that. She'd seen him as a powerful mentor, but now she viewed him as a puppeteer, manipulating his most gifted students to achieve what he'd never dared to try. She was herself, not a puppet.

Because she was her own person and not some mannequin to be shoved around according to her mentor's ambitions, she could rethink her career path. She could realize the value in teaching kids, although she'd learned the hard way not to push them into venues that didn't work for them. She could begin to value the gigs she booked even if they were within the state and not in some exotic location.

She had to face the truth. She pulled great satisfaction from performing in front of a crowd of Wyoming natives. A sophisticated crowd in an LA nightclub didn't excite her at all. Even Jackson Hole was a little rich for her blood, although she recognized the opportunities in such a cosmopolitan town.

Then why was she angling for a lucrative recording contract, a fifteen-city tour and international fame? She'd been taught to want that. She'd been conditioned to believe that if you had the necessary talent, you were obligated to take that ability as far as you could.

Her father had that kind of talent. She'd heard him play and he was easily as good as the big names. But he'd chosen a different path. At one time she'd viewed that as copping out, but she didn't see her father's decision that way now.

Success came in all sizes and shapes. Sometimes it flashed on the giant screen in Times Square. Sometimes it came in the form of enthusiastic applause from the crowd at the local Elks Club. Amethyst thought about how Jake measured success—a family saved from a house fire, a child plucked from a backyard swimming pool.

She thought about Professor Edenbury and the fire in his eyes as he'd dictated her marching orders. *Go out there and knock 'em dead, Ferguson! Make your old professor proud!*

A weight lifted from her shoulders as she realized that she didn't have to obey his marching orders, didn't have to live his dream. Instead she could live her own. She could stay in Sheridan.

The decision made her giddy with relief. She jabbered away with the registration clerk while checking into the hotel. Smiling, he agreed with her that Wyoming was a fabulous place to live. Then he gave her the room key and an envelope with her name on it.

Her heart leaped. Jake? She tore into it while she was still at the desk and glanced at the signature without reading the note. Not Jake. It was from the guy in charge of booking entertainment at the resort. Damn.

She stuffed the unread message into her purse and wheeled her suitcase over to the elevators. After she'd settled into her room, hung up her dress and taken off her shoes, she pulled the note out of her purse.

Amethyst—a guy from LA named Gerald Kincaid will be in the audience tonight. He's heard one of your demos and wants to talk with you. I gave him a table near the stage. Thought you'd want a heads-up.
Bob

IT HAD BEEN a busy night at the fire station with numerous calls, which was tough luck for the people involved but a blessing for Jake. If he'd had to sit around watching TV or playing cards, he'd have been tortured with thoughts of Amethyst. She'd been on his mind during every idle moment since leaving Sheridan, but tonight was worse because she was a short drive away.

So he'd welcomed the sound of the alarm because whenever he climbed on the truck, nothing else mattered. After an easily contained kitchen fire that was more messy than dangerous, he returned in a state of exhaustion, which was also welcome.

Sleep had been elusive the past few nights but maybe

he could sneak in an hour or two in the firehouse after a hot shower. As he was putting away his gear, his buddy Steve grabbed him by the shoulder.

"Somebody's here to see you."

"To see me?" He used the front of his T-shirt to wipe some of the soot from his face. "At three in the morning?"

"Yeah. A woman. Said she needed to talk to you. Chief stuck her in his office so you two could have some privacy."

Dear God. Had to be Amethyst. "Thanks."

His exhaustion vanished as adrenaline kicked in. Maybe she'd come to ask for the key to his apartment because she'd changed her mind about spending time with him. She might want another sexy encounter before they said goodbye forever.

He wished he had the willpower to reject the idea, but he'd take what he could get. He'd missed her like the very devil ever since driving away from Sheridan the day after Christmas.

Whenever he was working in the sooty stench of a fire, he forgot about Amethyst. But the minute the crisis had passed, his brain was flooded with images of her.

Seeing her again was like a mirage in the desert. He wanted to believe she was here but couldn't quite accept the reality of it.

Hurrying to the chief's office, he walked through the open door. Because he didn't know what to expect from this meeting, he closed it behind him.

She leaped up and tears glistened in her eyes. "Oh, Jake." Flinging herself into his arms, she peppered his grimy face with kisses. "I love you so much."

"I love you, too, but I'm filthy." Catching her around

the waist, he eased her away from him. "You'll ruin your sparkly dress."

"I don't care." She gazed up at him, her mascara smudged and her makeup streaked with tears. "I came over here as soon as I could, and you were gone, and I've been waiting, and I had the most horrible thoughts about something happening to you."

"Nothing's going to happen to me. I'm tough and I'm careful."

"I know, but...did you get the job in Sheridan?"

"I did, as a matter of fact. I start in two weeks."

"Good. That's so good."

He took a deep breath and tried to calm his racing heart. "Why are you here?"

She swallowed. "A talent scout from a recording studio came to my performance."

"Is that right?" He pumped as much enthusiasm into his response as he could manage. She'd come to share her good news and he would, by God, be happy for her. It was what she wanted. "That's great! Do you have an offer?"

"He made me one and—"

"That's terrific!" Love was so weird. His own heart was breaking but he could still feel joy for her. "You did it. Now you'll have—"

"Jake, I didn't take it."

The statement was like a smack upside the head. "Why not? Was it a crap deal?"

"No, it was a very good deal." She drew in a shaky breath. "That's what I came to tell you. I'm not going to LA. I want to stay in Sheridan."

He stared at her as he tried to process that. "But if you'd be earning money from the get-go, that takes away a big part of the risk. Why the hell aren't you going?" He had an awful thought. "Is something wrong with one of your parents?"

"No."

"Then why not go?"

"Because I don't want to. Professor Edenbury's dream is not mine." Smiling, she tucked a finger under his chin. "You'll catch a fly."

He closed his mouth but he was still stunned that she'd refused a contract. "Are you sure about this? Going there with no guarantees was one thing, but this deal is exactly what you wanted."

"I know. But on the drive over I realized that you were right. I've let Professor Edenbury's expectations have too much power over me. I love Sheridan, love being near my parents, love teaching my students, recording in my studio and living in that house. Why would I leave everything I love?"

"Beats me." He began to understand the enormity of her decision. And the rightness of it. This could be good, very good.

"I have a great life. And I'm telling you that because I'm not staying just because I want to be with you."

"I'm glad. Then you'd be trading your professor's expectations for mine."

"I promise that's not the case. But unless you've made other living arrangements, you can be my roommate if you want."

"Oh, I want." A surge of incredible joy made him forget about her sparkly dress and he pulled her close. Then he realized what he'd done and released her again. "Maybe this should wait until I'm—"

"Oh, no, you don't." She plastered herself against him.

"I realize you're on duty and all I can have is a kiss for now, but I'm hoping for more later. Lots more."

"Count on it." He lowered his head and brushed his mouth over hers. "I'm all yours."

"Then I have everything I could ever want."

"Me, too." He kissed her with tenderness, gratitude and as much passion as he dared. But mostly he kissed her with all the love in his heart.

Epilogue

MATT FORREST HAD made some very good friends during his three years in Tinseltown, but when he signed a
contract for his first major movie role, the two people he
most wanted to tell were a thousand miles away. Thank
God for cell phones.

He called his foster mother first because she was better at keeping her phone nearby. His foster father seldom
carried one while he handled his daily chores, but Rosie
liked being able to get calls wherever she happened to
be. She would love getting this one.

"Matt!" She sounded excited already.

"Hey, Mom! Are you at home?"

"I most certainly am and I've been on pins and nee-
dles waiting for the news. Did you get it?"

"I did!" He'd gone back to his tiny apartment to make
the call so they could hear each other. But he had to hold
the phone away from his ear for a while because the only
mother he'd ever known was going apeshit on the other
end. He sat there grinning while she whooped and hol-
lered. Yeah, this was the reaction he'd been looking for.

His friends would be happy for him. Some might

be jealous, but they'd be nice about it. The peripheral friends might wonder if they could capitalize on this development. But Rosie had pure joy going on without a single agenda.

Finally she wound down enough to have an actual conversation. "Okay, tell me everything."

"It's a Western. I think I mentioned that before."

"Yep."

"We'll be shooting on location in Utah beginning next month."

"How about Wyoming? We have great scenery for a Western and we'd get to see you!"

"Logistics. Economics. Utah's closer."

"I suppose."

"My costar is Briana Danvers."

"Wow! She's a big deal!"

"You're telling me. I still can't believe it. A big-budget film with a costar like Briana. I'm so flying you and Dad out for the premiere."

"Oh, my God, Matt, a *premiere*. This is incredible. Can I tell your dad or do you want to call him yourself? I know he's hard to get on the phone."

"You can tell him. You can tell anybody you want. It's official!"

"I can't wait to spread the word. Everyone is going to be so excited! Briana Danvers as a costar! I really like her, but I've had a crush on her husband for years. Talk about a gray fox. Clifton Wallace has it going on."

"People around here really love him, too. From what I hear, he's a class act. I'm hoping he visits the set once in a while. I've never met him but I admire his work."

"People are going to admire your work, too! This is

such wonderful news and you deserve it after all you've been through."

"Thanks, Mom. It feels really cool." He sighed. "Very cool."

"I'm sure it does. And I'll bet you have some other calls to make and some partying to do."

He laughed. "You know me too well."

"Go have fun! We'll celebrate the next time you make it home."

"We sure will. Give my love to Dad."

"I will."

"Love you, Mom."

"Love you, too, sweetie."

He disconnected and sat for a minute savoring the thrill of being able to make that phone call. He'd envisioned it for so long and had started to wonder if he was kidding himself about his prospects. At his lowest point he'd seriously considered moving back to Sheridan.

He could forget about that now. But this day would never have arrived without the years spent at Thunder Mountain Ranch and his foster parents' belief in him. Although they'd be proud of whatever he accomplished, he loved being able to give them something to really brag about. Their son was about to become a movie star.

* * * * *

*Vicki Lewis Thompson is moving
to Harlequin Special Edition!
Watch for Matt's story in the next installment of the*
THUNDER MOUNTAIN BROTHERHOOD *series,
published June 2017.*

COMING NEXT MONTH FROM

Available December 20, 2016

#923 DARING IN THE CITY
NYC Bachelors • by Jo Leigh

Luca Paladino moves into the town house he's renovating in Little Italy—a town house he thinks is empty. But he soon discovers a squatter upstairs, who turns out to be the woman of his dreams!

#924 TEMPTING THE BEST MAN
Wild Wedding Nights • by Tanya Michaels

When Professor Daniel Keegan runs into Mia Hayes at his best friend's bachelor party, their chemistry is off the charts. They're complete opposites, but she can't help tempting him to get a little wild...

#925 HOT PURSUIT
Hotshot Heroes • by Lisa Childs

Hotshot superintendent Braden Zimmer is surprised when beautiful, young Sam McRooney shows up to take over his arson investigation. Will their sizzling chemistry bring them together, or is it a deadly distraction?

#926 PUSHING THE LIMITS
Space Cowboys • by Katherine Garbera

Astronaut Hemi "Thor" Barrett is training at the Bar T Ranch to make the elite long-term mission crew. He can't afford to be hot for teacher, and survival instructor Jessie Odell is definitely raising his temperature...

REQUEST YOUR FREE BOOKS!
2 FREE NOVELS PLUS 2 FREE GIFTS!

HARLEQUIN®

Blaze

red-hot reads!

YES! Please send me 2 FREE Harlequin® Blaze® novels and my 2 FREE gifts (gifts are worth about $10). After receiving them, if I don't wish to receive any more books, I can return the shipping statement marked "cancel." If I don't cancel, I will receive 4 brand-new novels every month and be billed just $4.74 per book in the U.S. or $5.21 per book in Canada. That's a savings of at least 14% off the cover price. It's quite a bargain. Shipping and handling is just 50¢ per book in the U.S. and 75¢ per book in Canada.* I understand that accepting the 2 free books and gifts places me under no obligation to buy anything. I can always return a shipment and cancel at any time. Even if I never buy another book, the two free books and gifts are mine to keep forever.

150/350 HDN GH2D

Name _____ (PLEASE PRINT)

Address _____ Apt. #

City _____ State/Prov. _____ Zip/Postal Code

Signature (if under 18, a parent or guardian must sign)

Mail to the **Reader Service:**
IN U.S.A.: P.O. Box 1867, Buffalo, NY 14240-1867
IN CANADA: P.O. Box 609, Fort Erie, Ontario L2A 5X3

Want to try two free books from another line?
Call 1-800-873-8635 or visit www.ReaderService.com.

* Terms and prices subject to change without notice. Prices do not include applicable taxes. Sales tax applicable in N.Y. Canadian residents will be charged applicable taxes. Offer not valid in Quebec. This offer is limited to one order per household. Not valid for current subscribers to Harlequin Blaze books. All orders subject to credit approval. Credit or debit balances in a customer's account(s) may be offset by any other outstanding balance owed by or to the customer. Please allow 4 to 6 weeks for delivery. Offer available while quantities last.

Your Privacy—The Reader Service is committed to protecting your privacy. Our Privacy Policy is available online at www.ReaderService.com or upon request from the Reader Service.

We make a portion of our mailing list available to reputable third parties that offer products we believe may interest you. If you prefer that we not exchange your name with third parties, or if you wish to clarify or modify your communication preferences, please visit us at www.ReaderService.com/consumerschoice or write to us at Reader Service Preference Service, P.O. Box 9062, Buffalo, NY 14240-9062. Include your complete name and address.

HB15

Meet sexy NYC bachelor Luca Paladino from
DARING IN THE CITY by Jo Leigh,
on sale January 2017 from Harlequin Blaze!

Luca didn't get back to his new place until just after 8:00 p.m. It had turned blustery, and he rubbed his cold hands together as he entered the elevator.

Finally. He had his own apartment. Tomorrow his king bed and wide-screen TV would be delivered.

Ten minutes later he thought he heard the buzzer, but no way was the pizza he ordered here that fast. A moment later a scream rang out.

He grabbed the crowbar sitting on a pile of rags, his heart racing. It occurred to him that the scream didn't sound like a "help, I'm being assaulted" scream.

He moved closer to the door. Another scream, this time louder. It was coming from inside his apartment.

Luca glanced up the stairs. Goddamn Wes Holland hadn't moved out. Or he had, but he'd left a woman behind.

Cursing, he started up the staircase. As he moved stealthily down the hallway he heard her shouting. "Bastard" came in the clearest, followed by a wail.

He waited at the edge of the door, finally able to hear her words.

"How the hell does promising to pay me back do me any good?"

The tears and desperation came through loud and clear.

"That was all my savings," she said. "I hate you. You're such a coward, you won't even pick up."

Luca assumed the woman was talking about Wes and leaving him a voice mail. Had he really run off with her money?

He risked peeking inside the room. Luckily, the woman had her back to him. Lucky for him because it was a very nice view: the woman was wearing nothing but underwear.

Very tiny underwear.

Her bikini panties were pale blue, resting high on each cheek, just far enough to make him catch his breath. On top, he spotted the straps of her matching bra poking out from underneath a cascade of thick auburn hair.

He wondered what she looked like from the front…

She turned quickly, probably hearing his irregular breathing.

Now her scream was definitely of the "help, I'm being assaulted" variety.

He lowered the crowbar, noticing the two large suitcases behind her. "Hey," he said softly. "I'm not going to hurt you."

She waved her cell phone at him as she grabbed the nearest thing at hand—a pillow—and held it up against her semi-naked body. "I've already hit my panic button. The police will be here any minute."

"Good," he said, leaning his weapon against the door frame, trying hard to ignore the fact that she was hot. Certainly way too hot for that douchebag, Wes. "I'm anxious to hear you explain what you're doing in my apartment."

"*Your* apartment? You mean you own the one below?"

He nodded. "It's all one unit."

"But I have a key. And five days left on the rental agreement."

"What agreement?"

"My…" Her pause was notable, mostly for the look of fury that passed across her face. "My jerkface former business partner rented this place from the— From you, I guess. But I didn't think you lived here."

"Huh. Well, I think you might have been misinformed by Jerkface. I'm assuming you mean Wes Holland?"

Her whole demeanor changed from fierce guardedness to utter defeat. "Wait a minute. How do I know you're the real owner?"

"I understand you must be angry," he said, "but that doesn't change the fact that you'll have to leave."

"What? *Now?*"

"Well, no." It was already late, and he couldn't see himself throwing her out. "First thing tomorrow."

Pick up DARING IN THE CITY by Jo Leigh,
available in January 2017 wherever you buy
Harlequin® Blaze® books.

www.Harlequin.com

6040

Love the Harlequin book you just read?

Your opinion matters.

Review this book on your favorite book site, review site, blog or your own social media properties and share your opinion with other readers!

Be sure to connect with us at:
Harlequin.com/Newsletters
Facebook.com/HarlequinBooks
Twitter.com/HarlequinBooks